My Opic Observations

Jack Haines

Published by Rogue Phoenix Press
Copyright © 2013

ISBN: **978-1-62420-073-1**

Credits

Cover Artist: Designs by Ms G

Editor: Christine Young

Printed in the United States of America

OBSERVATIONS I HAVE MADE

Chapter One: HOSPITALITY, SWEET!

Have you ever noticed when you can least afford it; you end up begging someone to take your money, even though they don't really need it, and there is an obvious solution staring you right in the face?

An example of this is when you are having a beer in your favorite watering hole and you watch some poor schmuck empty his wallet into a video poker machine. You feel sorry for him the fifty-seven cents he's asking you for to buy a bullet to get over his addiction. The obvious solution to this situation is to stay in your seat, sit back and have another beer because you know the machines are cold tonight.

Armed with logic and clear thinking, you march over to the video poker area. This is where you will avenge the honor of Paul Bunyan and his fall to the tree cutting machine. MAN VS. MACHINE: Part Two; Well, three, if you count the guy who just left. However, there is a wrinkle in your plan. You are trying to slide your money into the machines blinking green mouth, but for some reason the machine does not accept your twenty. You openly curse the Ancient Chinese for inventing wrinkled paper money. Time after time you try to insert your money, only to have the machine spit it back out. With frustration building, you become temporarily insane. You are now fighting with a cold non-thinking metal box.

"Why will you not take my money? What do I have to do to get you to rob me? Fine! I'm going to a higher authority. I'm going to tell the bartender.

"I showed that machine!"

Why is the bartender rolling his eyes? You thank the bartender for trading your wrinkled twenty dollar bill for a crisp one. Simply point your crisp money toward the slot and it is slurped up like the last noodle on Spaghetti Night. Ha! You made it eat your money. You won! Fifty two seconds later it burps a thank you and you are walking back to your stool, without winnings. The machine did not need your money, but you forced it to take it. Victory!

I was offered an opportunity last spring that proves this out again; another Man vs. Machine contest. This time it started early on a Sunday morning. I woke up feeling ill and throwing up. The dark color made me quite concerned. By Monday morning, I had thrown up again and otherwise evacuated, as they say, the same color material until I was quite empty.

I knew this was not a good sign, but since I already planned to get my meds refilled the next day, I figured I could get it checked out then. Tuesday I went to the Indian Health Clinic, where I get my health care and monthly prescriptions refilled because I am diabetic and a bit hypertensive. I spoke to the head nurse who wrote a referral to get me in to see a gastroenterologist.

Wednesday morning I started my conversations with the "Gastro-Kids." You should understand at this point that the "Gastro-Kids" are part of the Community Hospital Complex LLC. The Community Hospital Complex LLC is a conglomerate of local doctors who also own the local hospital. They follow a very strict code, one established by their founders, Mr. Haney and Don Corleone: "We will tell you what you need and we just happen to have it right over here. You got a problem with that?"

I spoke on the phone with a very nice girl at the gastro-kids' office. She was very empathetic. She might have been new. The gastro-office is actually a suite of offices on the third floor of the North Wing of the Community Hospital Complex LLC. She listened to my story. She understood that I was in dire need of their services and that I had a referral from my clinic to get in to see a specialist. She weighed this against what she had been told to do.

She politely told me that I must go to the Community Hospital Complex LLC: Emergency Room Division to get a referral from them to get an appointment to see the gastro-kids. I momentarily disarmed her with the use of clear logic. "If I already have a referral, why would I need another one? My doctor is a real doctor. This referral is written on real paper. Okay, it may not be written on Community Hospital Complex: Emergency Room Division Referral Paper, but why would I want to spend at least half of tomorrow sitting next to some jittery guy in very dirty clothes who is holding his hand in pain to get something I already have?"

Not knowing the appropriate Mr. Haneyism, the nice girl said she would look into it and call me back.

At this time I realize that I am looking at the difference between twenty dollars in a bar's video poker area and a thousand dollars in ER fees. Although both are insatiable machines, the value of the stakes are quite dissimilar.

Since I am half German, I never know when to quit, but on the other hand, I am half German and like I have been told many times in my life, "...a tousand dollars is a tousand dollars." I slowed down and began looking at this from a different angle. This angle expanded rather than limited my vision.

I got out my phone book, looked down the road to the next town and found a gastro-guy that didn't belong to the Community Hospital Complex LLC. When I talked to the new nice girl, she said, "A referral? You can just walk in off the street. I can get you in Friday at three. Will that be alright?"

"Sweet!"

The next day, the first nice girl called me back. It sounded as though she was reading this message while kneeling in front of a Community Hospital Complex LLC flag with a totally gowned and masked surgeon on either side with an AK-47 and two bandoleers crossed under the stethoscope that draped their neck.

"We can get you an appointment in two weeks," she stated coolly. "Unfortunately, you still have to go to the Community Hospital Complex LLC: Emergency Division for a referral."

"Thank you for your concern, Nice Girl Number One, but I just got an appointment in the neighboring town for tomorrow at three."

"Oh, that's nice. I guess."

"Oh yeah! Real nice!"

Friday afternoon, my wife drove me down the road to the next town for my three o'clock appointment with Dr. Schmedley, the neighboring gastro-guy.

When I got out of the car, I could barely see because the sunlight was so bright it actually hurt my head. My legs were like lead and just walking to the building was more than I could do. We rode the elevator to the next floor to meet the doctor. Dr. Schmedley was a very nice man. He had his nurse run a few basic tests on me, and then we met in his office. He said that on Tuesday he would scope me, but in the meantime he instructed my wife to take me downstairs, put me in the car and carefully drive me across the street to the ER at the small town hospital.

She drove me to the drop off area and they were waiting for me at the door. They put me in a little room; the attendants were very nice to me. They asked me a million questions and examined me in more places than I knew I had. I was naked and in bed faster than a prom queen on her big night.

They were trying to explain to me that I had lost a lot of blood and my blood pressure was sixty over forty. I knew I was feeling pretty goofy even by my standards. My wife met up with me in my little room after filling out the paperwork. She was with me when I went to my new digs, ICU. Like the old joke, ICU is short for "I see you," because they do. Everyone does. There should be a sign on the door telling you to check your modesty. The ICU nurses were the best; they pumped me full of fluids: blood and saline. They watched me day and night for two days. I did my best to not wiggle very much since I was tethered down with two IVs, a BP cuff, O2 sensor, heart monitor leads and a catheter, need I say more?

During my stay, Dr. Schmedley stopped by to give me an endoscopy. He found a small hole in my esophagus. Just a small tear, probably caused by coughing, that he could fix with some medication, a pill that turned into gut putty that would seal up my little rupture.

Also during my stay I met two "hospitalists," Dr. Watson and young Dr. Jim. They both had a problem making eye contact with me. Dr. Watson and young Dr. Jim were young new age doctors. They were proud to be doctors in the small hospital. They proudly carried their special tools supplied by corporate sponsors: stereoscopes emblazoned with a pharmaceutical company's logo, multi-colored ball point pens with the name of the local drug store and a plastic pocket protector with the name of another company.

They were both concerned with my healthcare, maybe because they worked in the small hospital and had no patients of their own. They probably had time to sit around and second guess the choices of everyone they met. I know they were concerned about my healthcare choices because whenever they came to see me, they told me to stop taking one of my "meds." When they took me off insulin, I became alarmed.

Dr. Watson explained it this way, "Jack, you are taking old medicine. You may think you are feeling better but you are not. Look at you, you are the hospital. You need this brand of medicine. You need Shiny New Medicine." He reached into his pocket and pulled out his key ring. He rolled it around in his hand until he found a metal tag with the name "Shiny New" stamped into the metal. "See, Jack. Isn't that shiny?" he smiled in my direction, still making sure not to make eye contact. I could have sworn I saw Kool-Aid stains on the corners of mouth.

"But Dr. Watson, that looks expensive. I don't think my clinic carries that shiny brand."

His eyes rose up to the heavens for help on this objection. This was the part all doctors had a problem talking about. "Yes, Jack. Your clinic doesn't carry the shiny brand'." He now looks at his shoes, takes a deep breath and blurts out, "because, they are godless pony doctors who do not like you."

"Really? I always thought they were the perfect example of how socialized medicine could work in our crass corporate world."

"Exactly! So you see what I mean. You must remember, always use Shiny Brands for all your medical needs. We don't do bloodletting or chanting any more, not since God found Shiny Brands."

"Ohhh."

Sunday morning my wife brought my clothes. Ahhh, clothes. No more IVs. No catheter. No more feeling like John Lennon in that famous bed. After I was unplugged, I got dressed and sat on the edge of the bed waiting to be discharged. Dr. Watson stopped by to see me off, without actually looking at me. He was happy to see my wife. He gave her a list of things to do and not do. He looked over the top of her head to explain what had happened to me and how I would be as good as new, thanks to Shiny Brand Meds. He gave her a stack of prescriptions for all Shiny Brands.

I feel better today and still thank the ER gang and the ICU girls for saving my life.

I have since been back to my clinic and got back on my old fashioned meds. After two months, my blood sugars leveled off and I feel good. I still feed the video poker machines, but I think about it more. I think it will always be a struggle between man and machine. I prefer the machine that only asks for crisp money, not my soul and free will.

Chapter Two: A CHRISTMAS MIRACLE

It's funny how the holidays bring out the best in people or is it that we see how they really are. Many Christmases ago I learned more about people than I wanted to know at the time. Today with my old eyes, I see it in everyone.

In the early eighties I had a Christmas tree lot in Southern California. I picked out a thousand beautiful evergreen trees from my hometown in Oregon. I arranged for them to be freighted to South East LA. I drove a pick-up and camper down and had three days to get everything ready before the trees would arrive.

I rented a large tent and had it erected on the space I leased for the month in front of a closed supermarket. When my trees showed up, they were stored in the large tent. I constructed some racks to allow the trees to be displayed for the buyers. I used trees to barter for almost everything I needed and hired a couple neighborhood kids to work for me for the month after school.

We strung up lights for both decoration and for illumination. We had an area lit up by three flood lights that we used for our business area at night; it was at the end of a row of trees. The customers selected their trees. Bobby or I carried them to this area so that they could be bathed in the white light. This helped everyone envision how this tree could officiate over their Christmas Holiday Season. It always was magical.

After sharing several hundred Christmas dreams, I learned how to read my customers. Most chose the tree as a centerpiece in their house.

After the tree was selected, they needed several minutes to visualize how beautiful their holiday was going to be. We then would carry the tree to the family car and either put it in the trunk or secure it on top with twine. The family would jump into the car and they were off to enjoy their Happy Holiday.

As I said, most people are concerned with their tree selection, and then there were the people who are motivated by some other reasons.

I discovered something completely by accident, but since I saw it that one time, I have seen it thousands of times since in thousands of people. It is evil, not pure evil, just a streak. The width depends on the individual but the symptoms are the same. Once I saw it in my customers, I would use it for my own benefit. Why not? I discovered it and they would deny they had a streak of evil but they did and it worked every time.

One night about two weeks before Christmas, I had a family come to my tree lot. They seemed quite normal at first. They roamed through the lot looking for their perfect tree. Nothing I had was magical enough for them. The trees were too tall, too short, bald on the backside or had too many limbs on the back side. This had happened before.

Not knowing what their dream tree was supposed to look like, I wouldn't have been able to spy it in the field and mark it for the farmer to cut for me. There might not have been enough room on the truck to accommodate the grandiose greenery that would accent their foyer adequately. I bid them good luck in their search elsewhere and turned to help another customer.

I heard a scream behind me. I spun around to see that same family talking to Bobby under the flood lit area. Bobby was shaking his head and pointing at me.

"We want this tree!" the man declared triumphantly. "But your boy here says there is a problem!"

Under the three flood lights, bathed in glory, stood the most beautiful tree I had ever seen.

"What's the problem?" I asked.

"Your boy," the man sputtered.

"Bobby?"

"Yeah, your boy, Bobby, said I can't buy this tree. What kind of place are you running here? We have laws here in California! Consumer laws! I could sue you for everything you own. You Oregonians are all alike."

I looked at Bobby. He looked like he was ready to cry. "What happened, Bobby?" I asked.

"I was holding that tree for a guy who came in earlier," Bobby choked out. "The guy said he had to go to the bank to get some money. He asked if I could hold it until 7:30. I wrote it on this piece of paper." Bobby reached for a small note that was doubled over a small branch and stapled to itself. He opened the note and handed it to me. He mopped his brow with his sleeve and stepped back out of the light.

In block letters the note read, "HOLD UNTIL 7:30, B.".

"If he wanted it, he would be here by now!"

I almost forgot the litigator and his family. They were standing next to the tree. They were already dreaming about Christmas morning. They would be opening presents while dad was handcuffing Santa in the kitchen and waiting for the police to arrive to bust him on breaking and entering charges. I looked at my watch; 7:27. I looked over to Bobby. I gave him a look of reassurance. He wouldn't be sued just before Christmas.

"Bobby, did you take any money to hold the tree?"

"No, Jack."

"My watch says 7:35! He didn't put down a deposit. Legally that tree is mine!"

"Yay!" screamed the kids.

"My hero!" the wife must have sighed to herself, pride welling up in her bosom.

"I don't know what to say. The time is up and there was no deposit, you can buy the tree," I concurred. "Bobby, could you help them with the tree, please?"

"Sure, Jack."

The whole family was shouting as they danced out to their car.

I took a moment to process what just happened. I read about certain bird species that wait for another bird to build its nest then forcibly take over the nest and lay its eggs therein. I never thought people would do that. It's not out of necessity that people would take another person's Christmas tree. It's not because they are too tired or unimaginative to dream their own Christmas dream. It is simply the evil in them.

It surfaces when there is a chance for someone to steal the dream of another. If the tree was being held for someone, that meant they had dreamt about how that tree would complete their Christmas. To take that tree, would be to dash their dreams and to enjoy that tree even more than any other tree would be lazy and evil.

You might think I'm jaded or misinterpreting the facts. I'm not and I can prove it.

From that moment on I had Bobby place a tree under the light bath and staple a small note on it with a request to hold it until fifteen minutes ago. As the dreamers would circle around the lot seemingly unimpressed, I would approach them and point out how they could have any tree on the lot except one, that one. At that point they quit dreaming and started scheming. They had to have that tree. They had to have that dream.

It worked. It worked every time. Bobby and I re-enacted the tree holding every hour of the day for the next two weeks. We giggled all the way back from the cars. It was funny but it really isn't funny after all.

Chapter Three: TAKE THIS DOWN

Last week I responded to an ad asking for a writer to offer an example of their style for a blog. They wanted a "Hard-hitting, no prisoners taken, stark look" at where they live for a famous blog site. "Bold, Blatant, Brutally Honest" was their slogan.

I sat down and produced two hundred and fifty words of what I thought was pretty clever stuff.

I wrote:

"Take off your watch, leave your I-Phone on the bus, crank up Verdi on your I-Pod, squint your eyes a little and be transported back in time. It works every time you take a winery tour in the beautiful Willamette Valley of Oregon.

"After the ubiquitous lesson on how wine is made, go outside the barn-like structure, sit on the ground and soak in the view of the vineyard turning young grapes into mature grapes. You can imagine yourself in ancient Italy.

"You, of course, have to begin drinking as soon as you arrive and distance yourself from the other winery tourists. Since tours are held year-round in the Willamette Valley, this is easy because it is probably raining and by sitting on the ground, your pants are now wet. Most people will leave you alone except for those offering to give you CPR.

"The time travel is marvelous and will last as long as your Chianti holds out. Stumble back up the Appian Way to the barn/wine storage area, help yourself to cubes of cheese from the bowl by the front door and grab a baguette on the way back to the bus.

"The next stop in your wine tour is just up the road. Change Verdi for Bach and get ready for some Riesling.

"The tour will take in three or four wineries per day. It is recommended you take the tour on Saturday so you can use Sunday to relax from all that time traveling and dry your pants before you go back to work on Monday.

"There are many companies offering tours from all directions, consult the Yellow Pages or there might be an APP for that "

The next day I received an e-mail stating that although he liked my style, the niche group was not being served by my piece. He wanted to encourage people to move here based on my Bold, Blatant and Brutally Honest description of my homeland.

The part that disturbs me is why would I want to invite people to move to my region to vie for the few jobs that are being held for the people who already live here and need the work? Who is this niche group? Young professionals who surf the net?

No way! I don't think I can do that. I think I'll just do what I normally do; throw rocks at young professionals who want to swoop into my territory and take over.

Then I started thinking…

This was the latest example in a long line of revelations that I chose the wrong path to follow. I remember in school during career week, I had lofty dreams of becoming a "Freelance Writer." First of all, I liked the sound of it. Freelance, it had an adventurous and romantic sound to it. I could visualize myself working in a small second story office most likely next to Philip Marlowe. I could visualize my name printed on the frosted glass door: "JACK MARLOWE, Word Smith". The small waiting room was packed with dames, all nervously smoking Chesterfields and waiting their turn to talk to me. Molly, my "Girl Friday," had taken all of their names and sat them in alphabetical order.

I was in my office, just past the door marked PRIVATE. Sitting behind the Olivetti on my big oak desk, I'm hammering out the sensitive parts of the story being told to me by Carmen Sternwood. She sat in front of me, legs crossed, while she spilled her guts in great detail about some indiscretion she just committed. I offered her a shot. She gulped down the Old Crow like a teamster. I lit up her smoke and sat back down behind my forty-seven key Wurlitzer. "You just keep talking, Baby. I'll pound this out till my fingers bleed." She couldn't stop her tear-filled confession. It was hot. It was the kind of story that would make Mitzie, the fan dancer at Carmichael's, blush. It had everything, everything but an ending.

Now that was' Freelance Writing' to me. Boy, was I naïve?

What is closer to the truth is that the 'Free' in Freelance doesn't stand for freedom; it probably stands for Free-To-Work. Free-To Work is a clever play on words, more than likely created by a Freelance writer in Arizona, Florida or Nevada. If you lived in these states, you would call it Free-To-Starve, they do and they do.

Freelance Writing, I now think, is a direct descendent of Freelance Scribing. This evokes the image of me being shackled to a table on the fourth floor of the Church Tower. This time I have a small plaque covered with candle wax on my desk. Engraved on the plaque is BROTHER JACCOBUS, SCRIVENER. Next to the desk is a small lad holding a tome on his back for me to copy. Callused fingers sharpen my quill as I tell the boy to quit wiggling. While I dream of carbon paper, he is dreaming of removable type and offset printing. Lazy bum!

The ugly truth is that writing for pay is neither romantic nor adventuresome. It does not help the poor and uneducated tell their story or document their will.

Today, these ads for writers are for writers to manipulate the poor and uneducated into buying something or thinking a certain way. The jobs for writers today are to help some guy sell new Snake Oil on the internet. Writing is not the only thing they seek. They want someone who can also put together a functional pop-up.

The days of dreaming of having a weekly column like Royko or Barry are all but gone; then it hit me. These guys were not freelancers, they were Feature Writers. It was my misconception of the meaning of freelance that led me into a place of daydreaming of becoming an accomplished Freelancer not a Feature Writer. I guess Freelance just sounded adventuresome.

Now I can read these ads and not worry whether my similes and metaphors will be used for good or evil. I will just write for myself.

Chapter Four: CLINICALLY PROVEN

Have you ever noticed how TV commercials and infomercials seem to be grasping to the point of being quite preposterous? I was sitting in my favorite chair, watching one of my favorite TV shows. I might have drifted off a little because I soon realized my show had ended some time ago. I was in the middle of an infomercial. It didn't take long to figure out that the studio audience must have been handpicked. This audience was all women. They were all in their thirties. They were all very excited about whatever product was being highlighted.

Because of that sleep thing I had been going through, I didn't hear what the moderator had said. What I did hear were the oohs and ahhs of seventy-five women

"No, No!" I heard myself moaning. I quickly woke up and looked around the room. Good, I was by myself.

The women were still oohing. What could possibly be that good? Now I'm paying very close attention. Some of the women were hugging imaginary lovers as they moan. Their eyes roll back in their heads as they squirmed in their chairs.

Was this a personal product? No, it was a beauty product. It was a new lipstick.

15

The moderator speaks, "...and it's clinically proven to make your lips not just look larger but grow larger."

"Oooh, Aaah!"

Now this is the part that makes my head hurt. I understand that the idea of having seventy-five women agreeing on anything, not just once but for thirty minutes, is more than likely impossible. The product people want you to believe the women are in agreement, but if you are like me and have a hard time grasping that foreign concept, they will trump any argument by stating it was clinically proven.

Scientifically proven in a clinic? What kind of clinic? Where are these clinics? I have never heard of a lip fulfillment clinic.

If you watch TV as much as in do, you will also come to the conclusion there must be thousands of these facilities across America. Hidden in plain sight or in some unmapped areas just outside of town, these clinics prove the effectiveness of thousands of products on our shelves today.

Not just lipstick but hair growing ointment, hair removal ointment, male and female scents, male and female deodorants, male performance and female enhancement, performance and hygiene products are tested and proven, according to the product sellers.

Now we all remember the early eighties when, due to activists' outrage, the laboratories were shut down all over America because the scientists were using defenseless animals on which to test products. Pigs and monkeys were dressed up in dresses. Beauty products were applied liberally then the test subjects were placed in a school gymnasium. The lights were dimmed and slow dance music was piped into the gym.

One by one the test subjects were asked to dance by another group of test subjects. The subjects that were not asked to dance were photographed by scientists; the checklist of products was matched to a master list. Data was entered into a giant computer. The looks of curiosity on the faces of the scientists coupled with the shame of not being asked to dance caused the test subjects to have inferiority complexes, according to the activists. The activists knew the pain of not being asked to dance and could not allow others the self-doubt they had in high school. They could remember the nights crying themselves to sleep.

"We cannot mistreat our four legged brothers and sisters. The scars! The scars! Stop the experiments now!"

They whipped up the emotions of average or maybe below average Americans with their campaign. Who can forget the photograph of the awkward looking young pig wearing a pink tutu with garish red lipstick smeared on her lips? Tears welled up in her eyes as in the background we could see a chimpanzee laughing and pointing at the pig. When the photograph hit the cover of Newsweek, the laboratories were locked up. Many people claim the researchers went to Mexico where animal abuse laws are less strict and the average person has more pressing things to be concerned with in their daily life.

Perhaps these abandoned laboratories were converted into clinics. Since clinics deal with people, not animals, the "trials" are tests on humans. How would that work?

The technology of today is by far superior to that of the eighties. Hidden cameras, night-vision goggles and GPS systems all must be part of the clinical trial process. All to help the product sellers to obtain that coveted "Clinically Proven" status.

The people of the Downtown Mission are trying to keep a lid on a brewing social scandal about the disappearances of some of our homeless citizens. Some insiders say trial "assistants" are being recruited from the downtown area with the promise of free beauty products and a bottle of "Mad Dog."

I saw on the internet last week a story about a town in Pennsylvania that reported zombies roaming the streets after dark, terrifying the people of the town. This story was quickly removed and deemed a hoax.

Was it really a hoax or was there a Cover Girl Cover Up? Maybe the story didn't report that there was a clinic on the outskirts of town. Maybe there was an experiment and dance at the clinic that night. Poorly dressed individuals who are testing a sturdy, all weather hair gel, not so sensitive deodorant, two part epoxy tooth polish, poorly designed incontinence products and a new garish red lipstick were running away from the shame of not being asked to dance could have been mistaken for zombies. It's possible.

It's as possible as getting seventy-five women agree on anything.

Chapter Five: CHANGING ONE'S HABITS

The problem with dieting is that it will change your life if you let it, which is what my wife says it is supposed to do. I understand, but I don't have to like it. It took me all this time to get to where I am, and I accepted and hung on to many bad habits along the way.

I quit smoking twice; the first time for nine years and now, the second time, for seven and a half years. It was a life changing episode that was good for me, so says my day-time brain. My day-time brain knows that I quit but my night time brain still plays dreams of me burning one now and then, hanging out with the cool kids out in the lean-to outside my favorite bar.

I know these dreams concern my wife because she bought pastel colored linens for our bed. I asked her why. She said she didn't like the smell of burning feathers in the middle of the night. I told her to just take all of the matches out of the bedroom. She said that I would probably just dream up a Zippo and she would have to buy more pillows.

My doctor likes the results of my new life style change; I think he hangs my 'A1c' blood sugar test on his refrigerator.

My wife has taken charge of food production and distribution. The product is more colorful but the size is understandably smaller. Because it is smaller, she learned a trick involving smaller food plates, thus making the portion to look larger than it actually is. It is a visual trick on one's brain.

My brain, however, drifts back to fifth grade when we had an assembly. Assemblies were our entertainment back then at school. We only had five TV stations and one of those was Educational TV and we avoided that one.

We were sitting on the floor in the gymnasium and our entertainment was a large sweaty man in a tuxedo. Behind him was a large banner; written in green glitter was his name, REGINALD THE AMAZING. We were beside ourselves with excitement. This was entertainment and it was in color, another problem with our TV system.

We were going to be amazed, the banner foretold that. The title REGINALD THE AMAZING was written in an arc with green glitter, but what was really amazing was the banner builder didn't have enough room for the G. it was slightly smaller and underneath the N. What was even more amazing than that was we didn't care. We were in an assembly, no studying math.

He sweated and stuttered through forty-five minutes of tricks. We applauded and "Yayed" every time his hands went up which indicated the end of an amazing illusion. We understood our role because we had seen amazing magic before; we were almost sixth graders.

There was, however, a third grader in the first row on the far right side. He had a great location to watch the show. It was not so great for Reginald. When Reginald shot his sweaty hands in the air after a particularly amazing trick involving a vanishing coin, the third grader, with his view from the side, blurted out, "It's in his pocket! He put it in his pocket!"

Reginald's face got red. He began stuttering even more than before. He used one of his amazing colored kerchiefs to wipe the top of his sweaty bald head and put it in his pocket on top of the amazing coin. Amazing as it sounds, we didn't care.

Sometimes, I feel like that third grader, I see the coin go into the pocket. I see the plates get smaller at dinner time, but unlike the third grader, I don't yell out and point. I understand my role and I stick to the script. The proof is in the ten percent of me that has disappeared. Smaller more colorful portions help me out and only occasionally does my night time brain give me Biscuit and Gravy dreams. I only got a bit concerned last week when my wife asked me where I stored the poker chips.

Although this new life style is taking over, I am not a fanatic. I didn't stop drinking beer, but now I only do it on weekends and pay day.

The other night we went to one of our old haunts. After reassuring our old buddies that we hadn't moved away, we got to sit back and enjoy our beer.

Things seemed to have changed a bit in our absence. The young people from the alternative music crowd that used to have weekend concerts three doors down are no longer showing up for a shot or two before the show. I used to enjoy talking to the members of the groups before the shows. They were quite famous in the music underground and I followed them on line. They lost their lease and took the show back to Portland.

Since nature abhors a vacuum, the young people's stools have been taken over by some local farmers who stop in on their way home for a couple shots, a little video poker and some music on the juke box.

I try not to act overly inquisitive ever but especially not in a bar. I feel it is better to only observe than to get involved. These guys were starting to push my buttons without even knowing it. I have always stated that all I ask for of a bar is to be a quiet oasis for me and my wife to sit back, relax and have a couple beers, no drama, just quiet and an occasional baseball game on the TV.

These new guys must have started at noon because they were well oiled at six. They started shouting, cursing and arguing over who chose better music. It soon escalated into a small brawl. There were three of them but it seemed that they were fighting three different battles from three different directions; each man strongly defended his different point of view. They punched and poked, spit and swore, twisted beards and gouged eyes. I have seen some great fights in my day and this looked like it was going to be one of them. Finally, Josie the bartender broke up the fight and told all to go home. They apologized to Josie, put on their black wide brimmed hats and helped each other outside. They each climbed into their own black buggy, whistled, pointed their roan west, crossed the bridge and headed home. One more beer for us and we were on our way home, chuckling as we went.

With five sevenths of our lives stuck steadfastly in sobriety, the on goings at our watering hole seems a bit odd now. It probably wouldn't have been so odd in the old days, or if it did, we wouldn't be third graders about it. We knew our roles.

Chapter Six: THE SLOW ECONOMY

Last night I was complaining to my wife how I just can't get started on one more writing project. I can't get behind a topic I feel passionate for. I was all dried up. I was doing exactly as I did before: sitting at my desk in front of my computer, behind me the television produces background noise to help keep my brain from gelling. Coffee does seem to help percolate my brain juices which will guide my fingers over the keys.

Blank Screen, Blank Screen, Blank Screen.

"...they say because of budget cuts, the city might be forced to shut down the library."

What? I now realize the television is broadcasting a little louder than normal. I can actually understand what is being said. Hearing is one thing, understanding is quite another. Why would they shut down the library?

The economy; in a slow economy, frilly things like learning must be removed from our grasp. Now everything we need to know will be sent to us by Rupert Murdoch. That's so nice of him.

I just have one issue with that. I know that the economy is slow, but let's not use it as a catch-all excuse for the failings of others. How many times do we see on the news someone talking to the reporter by sticking their head out from their SUV to excuse some transgressor for doing evil based on the slow economy.

"I know that young man robbed the bank in the nude then had his way with that herd of water buffalo but, you know, it is a slow economy."

They have nothing to do with each other. It really takes all I have not to write in all CAPS when I hear this, but what is worse is when they break away from the woman in her SUV and the news anchor states, "So there you have it, another casualty of the slow economy."

GRRR

"Now in a related story:"

Related? Nothing here is related!

"Due to economic shortfalls and in an effort to lower payroll expenditures because of overtime pay differential, the Pope announced today that from now until further notice, midnight mass will be held at eleven o'clock. The pontiff read from a prepared statement and did not stay to take questions. He did hint though, that if these cost cutting efforts do not stabilize the financial hemorrhaging, the church management would be forced to outsource to third world countries. The Pope left unanswered some questions shouted from the media to the rumor that many of the Church's more minor Sacraments are already being outsourced to China, Korea and India. As heard on this secret recording, the Vatican may be sending confessions by phone to outside agencies."

"Why do I have to use this phone? Aren't you just on the other side of the screen?"

"Yes, I mean No. I am…at my house…and…I am all by myself. The telephone is necessary to talk to me…at my house."

"All by yourself? It sounds like you are in a room full of people."

"Yes, I mean No. I am…watching my television. I am watching my favorite American television program…BONANSAI."

"Do mean BONANZA? That hasn't been on in decades."

"Yes, I mean No, I am watching my other favorite American television program...LUCY."

"Okay, let's get this started."

"Okay. Welcome Mister Sinner. I am Mister Father...Brian O'Reilly."

"Oh, really?"

"No, I am pretty sure it is O'Reilly...would you prefer...Flanagan?"

"What?"

"...I will state a particular sin and you will tell me if you took part in this sin this week. Then you will tell me if it is favorite sin, not so favorite or never favorite sin. If you wish you can press one for YES or nine for NO. Do you understand?"

"Yes, I underst..."

"Did you say...sex?"

"What? No I said..."

"That will be three HAIL MARYs. Please, swipe your credit card through the card reader and press number three. Thank you for calling your confession into Our Lady of the Ganges: Confession/Absolution Station; Mister Jason Johnson, President."

"What?"

CLICK...BUZZ!

"Hello?"

Well, it must be true. Who could make up this stuff? This is FOX not CURRENT.

Chapter Seven: TIME FOR A CHANGE

I'm not very scientific. It's probably better that way. When I watch golf on TV, my mind wanders to how I wish I had a time machine. I don't know much about time travel, I know even less about time machines. If I had one, I could put it my garage. I might need to get an additional power outlet, maybe two hundred and twenty volts. I would use it completely for amusement purposes only.

I am sure there are all kinds of rules to time travel: no checking out Final Four games before placing a wager at the local pub, no changing world history and no erasing things on Face Book after you've already posted it. I am certain I could follow the rules up to a point.

Like I said earlier, my problem arises when I watch golf on TV.

I grew up watching professional golf on TV and I was introduced to the etiquette of the game by watching and listening Chris Schenkel whispering his observations into his oversized microphone. It was as though Chris were standing between Arnie, his caddy and you at the tee box. His voice was hushed as he would describe to us the club selection and wind direction at every stroke set-up. One could hear the swoosh of the club, the smack of the ball and the polite and subdued applause of the gallery. This etiquette was reinforced every weekend during the golf season for every year of my youth. Golf courses were quieter than church.

Things change, which is why I wish I had a time machine. There are, however, some questions I still have about the physical properties and restrictions of the machine. It would probably depend on which brand you bought. I could more than likely only afford to buy a low-budget model; it might have fewer bells and whistles.

I still have a couple questions: if I take a gun with me, can I only select a time period in which guns are already invented? I also wonder if I would take one of those five hour energy drinks just before I traveled and went back into time. How would I calculate how many hours of energy I would actually have? Should I only drink half of it for two and a half hours, or would it give me only half the energy for five hours?

I know you are probably rolling your eyes or hiding your loved ones, but please, hear me out. My cause is noble and I think you will agree.

Let's say I buy a PHILCO TIME PORTAL 2.0. I've got it set up in my garage and I have a pocket full of quarters to get back home. If I go back in time far enough I can find five generations of people before the birth of anyone. I would locate and shoot the ancestors of the guy who started that obnoxious yelling 'IN THE HOLE" every time someone tees off, chips, putts or stops to tie his shoe. I know the machine would pay for itself in remote control replacement fees alone.

I can also see myself going back in history to save HISTORY, THE HISTORY CHANNEL that is. I used to watch THE HISTORY CHANNEL religiously every day. I used to consider myself a fan of history. I watched and learned American History, World History, Ancient History, Planetary History and Cosmic History. I enjoyed every program they aired.

So now I will go back in time and would hunt down the forefathers of the guy who decided that a series about those lumber jack guys was: A, a part of history and B, entertaining. The story could have been easily covered in one program like they masterfully did with The History of Prom Dresses or The History of Pocket Lint.

Now that this type of program exists, we have to endure all of the spin-offs on this concept of tough guys in the working arena from all corners of the country, some of which I believe might be made up. If not, how can they justify Cajun Worm Ranchers, Brooklyn Garment Tag Fasteners, Alaskan Mukluk Gummers and Northeastern Sap Wranglers?

The premise for these shows is the same: competing companies vie for a gentleman's bet of seven dollars as to which company can work harder, faster and with the least regard for safety than the others or implode trying. Each company is saddled with a toothless old-timer trying to show the "Greenhorn," Bobby, how they used to do this dangerous job in the old days before safety laws and a hypertensive boss who need those seven dollars more than oxygen.

The dialog is always the same:

"Bobby! Git your bleeping bleep out there and pick up the bleeping bleep before I put my bleeping boot in your bleeping bleep.

History? I don't think so. Entertaining? No way!

I am sure this genre has its followers, like the people who think Richard Simmons is Gene's little brother or WWF is real. I'm sorry, I got carried away. I might have had too much energy drink. I told you it was hard to calculate.

The one thing I did learn about time travel is that if I thank you for reading my rant when I write it, it will carry into the future and be just as grateful today, when you read it, as when I wrote it in the past.

Thank You!

Chapter Eight: CLASS REUNION

It was a wonderful weekend. It was the weekend of my class reunion. I truly had a wonderful time. I talked to old friends that I hadn't seen in twenty years. It took all I had not to get emotional. Some of my friends could not reunite with us. They had passed. Passing is probably the only great escape from the class reunion. It's excusable and unavoidable.

The antithesis of escaping a class reunion is dropping in on a class reunion of someone else. I have a buddy whose ex-wife dropped in on his reunion. She never attended his high school, not one day. She did at one time, attend school in the same town that he did and made a couple friends before the high school years. This was considered the same as being an alumnus, I guess. I followed the progress of my friend's weekend from a distance. Poor bastard! His ex kept walking past him and greeting his current wife as though he was wearing his invisible suit. Both days of the function she was his wife's best friend. She sat with her junior high buddies peaking, snickering, whispering and pointing. It was so junior high.

Some things change, some things never change. I was talking with a friend of mine whose name happens to be the same as mine, Jack. Along comes Amish Andy.

"Look", he said. "Two Jacks!"

"Yes, it looks like you've got openers, Amish Andy".

Blink. Blink.

"You know, a pair of Jacks?"

Blink. Plus pursed lips.

"You know, 'Jacks or better to open,' Amish Andy"

This time it was two blinks, pursed lips and head scratching.

"Poker?"

Eyes blinking independently and alternately, pursed lips, knitted brow and hand on the back of the head, trying to keep it from popping off with this overload of confusing gibberish.

"Cards?"

"I've got to go, Jack and Jack. Owww."

"See ya, Amish Andy. Hmm."

I saw a collection of wives of alumni sitting a table. They seemed to know each other from other gatherings. They looked similar to each other. Kind of stringy hair, same off white tee shirt, missing teeth (not many, just enough so you would notice when they smiled or said any word containing an 's'). Like the one that talked to me, "Thay, thugar. Ith your thither thill a nurth?"

"No, my sister is a secretary for a sociologist at The University of Syracuse but stays in Schenectady."

"Ohh"

Everyone was friendly and because they made the effort to show up, you could tell they were happy to be there. You could hear the sound of rusty wheels spinning as they tried to figure out who they were talking to and then try to remember if they ever liked them back in high school. Twice, I saw people spin on their heels as the fog cleared, and they remembered the person they were talking to was their sworn enemy in school. Eventually, they got back together, realizing whatever it was that held them apart was not that great. Old age has a lot to do with that.

Ernesto, our foreign exchange student from Guacamala showed up. It seems that after high school, he was sent to military school and then the Navy, all here in the US. I always thought that was funny because we all knew Guacamala had no coast line. He became a fighter pilot and returned to his country. Soon he became the new Presidente of Guacamala.

He was re-elected for thirty years. He was very popular with his people, even though he really didn't spend much time in his own country. He spent a lot of time testifying in one Congressional Sub-Committee or another. You know I just have basic cable, but whenever I saw him on C-SPAN, he spoke with an accent and a slight lisp. He didn't have either of those this weekend. He did have a very nice looking motorcycle and a very nice looking date/niece.

Being Presidente must be a pretty good gig.

Some guys just weren't the guys I hung out with. One of those guys was Martin Winslow. Martin always hung out in the shop area. Martin was in the Ag. Club. Actually Martin was the Ag. Club. He went on to Aga Aga U., the nearby Ag. University and was named National Ag. Club President: with Clusters for life. He became rich and famous after he invented a seed that produced a self-mowing lawn. He sold the seeds to football and soccer fields all over the world. He lost his fortune after he lost the patent on the seed and the Chinese began production of the seeds. He was also investigated by a Senate Sub-Committee investigating a mass exodus of lawn care people back to Guacamala.

I soon got tired of telling my story: Yes, I am now retired, No, I enjoy doing nothing, Yes, that is quite unusual for me to have long hair now. I did not want to tell anyone that I now spend my time writing short rants and looking for an outlet for them that is just as quirky as I am. So, sometimes I would look left and then right, bow my head low, cup my hand to the side of my mouth and say:

"Former Astronaut. Yeah, the Moon"

"CIA Guy. Yeah, Agent"

"Lion Tamer."

"Inventor. Yeah, you know that thing you see on T.V."

"Stunt Double for Florence Henderson."

"I'll tell you later..."

"The Pope. Domini, Domini, Equity"

"Professional Bowler."

"I invented beer."

For some reason, I would always show up with a new spouse at each of these events. When I did all of my old buddies would want to be sure she knew all the goofy things we did back in the day. These guys are really your friends. I should know, this happens to me at every reunion.

Some guys don't say anything about the past, hoping you would forget seeing their picture on America's Most Wanted.

There was a girl taking pictures that she was willing to sell to you for ten dollars. I think she said this before she took the picture so you wouldn't goof up the shot and waste ten bucks on a picture of you trying to explain what a digital camera was to Amish Andy.

Blink

I can now prove there is evolution. At this reunion, Wendell, the party guy, was in the parking lot with his same old van. Only this year, out of the back, he was featuring Viagra.

As people get older, they want to carry less baggage with them and that means fewer secrets. I was informed by this girl that she was hoping I would have asked her out long ago.

I thought for a second and remembered that she was married when she was fourteen and at sixteen she had five kids. I would have had to ask her out when we was twelve but my Schwinn didn't have a side car.

Probably the saddest people at the reunion were the unfortunate ones who had very trying times throughout their lives. Bad luck, bad choices and bad relationships all led to the long road of addiction and the longer road to redemption. But they are okay now. They are no longer addicted. They have everything they need in the Lord. The Lord helped them kick drugs. The Lord is helping them find a job. The Lord helped them get a ride here today. The Lord helped them get this cool tee shirt, black with a picture of the Lord on the front and the phrase "Jonesin' for Jesus" on the back. At least they aren't addicted any more.

Now days, you can contact anyone on the World Wide Web. The people learned about the function on a social site. The restaurant we met at should have been looking for the e-mail that mentioned the day and time of the event. We had two months advanced notice where the function was being held. The restaurant seemed like they had none. At least seventy five people packed this tiny bar and grill. They were breaking in a new girl, ran out of top shelf booze a 5:05 and blew a keg of beer at 5:06. To the credit of the skeleton crew, they found a higher gear and were able to handle the crowd.

All things considered, the weekend rolled out a little better than expected. I would do it again. As it turns out I just found out we reserved the same cafe for our next reunion, in ten years. I heard the waitress just gave her notice.

Your buddies are always going to be your buddies no matter how much time elapses between visits. Reunions help reinforce that concept.

People you meet at reunions are always kinder than they were in real life. My wife and I have been offered a barn raising, a new back yard, a side car for my Schwinn and a trip to Guacamala. We might take it in ten years.

I think we should thank some of our corporate sponsors for the weekend:

The World Wide Web; makers of a better place in which to live thanks to those magical communication boxes.

Step Twelve Boot Company; footwear for the quitter in you.

Electronic Jewelry Extension Systems; "So you can go the extra mile,"

Jesus Does It Sports Wear; your savior in iron transfer clothing.

Thouth Thalem Thpeach Therapy; it goes without thaying.

Tia Juana Farmacia Distribution Compania; makers of the new and improved elder wonder drug Viagko, the half Viagra, half Gingko supplement. "It gives you something you've been looking for and the ability to remember what to do with it when you find it."

And:

Your local Junior High School; makers of memories and bonds that logic just can't break.

OUT AND ABOUT WITH JACK AND RUTH

Chapter One: SERVICE ANIMALS

"I would like to buy some poison, please."

"Lady, this is a pharmacy not a hardware store," explained the man in the white smock. He pushed up his glasses with his index finger. He smiled as he looked down toward her small frame. "We don't carry rat Poison."

"No, Honey, it's for my husband."

In another part of the store I heard:

"I hope you like this book, Herb. I think you complained every other page of that mystery you bought last week."

"It was so predictable, Brenda. I knew who did it from the first line. Honestly, they'll print any crap they find now days."

"Times are tight now, Herb. It's not like the old days."

"Oooh!..."

As I walked through the store I could only think about how much more the same prescription cost today than it did even two years ago. I signed for my purchase and walked outside into the rain which was still in progress. The wind picked up and blew a small handful of rain into my face. The water came off the awning in front of the store.

I heard someplace, maybe on TV, that things are not like the old days. Boy, they knew what they were talking about. I turned left and walked down the empty sidewalk. I used the little white bag to try to keep the rain off my glasses. With my head bent over, I had to look over the top of my glasses to find our car parked on the side of the street. My wife was behind the wheel waiting for me. I hopped in the passenger side. "Let's go for pizza, Baby."

My wife carefully drove across town to our favorite pizza parlor. We entered, ordered our pie, picked up some beer and found a table in a far corner of the dining room. We always sit facing each other. We watch people as a hobby and take turns sitting in the seat with the view. Today was her day to watch and report.

Everything seemed to be text book about the crowd today.

There was the ever present family from the country: Mother and stair-stepped blond children, eleven years through eleven weeks, all twelve of them. Twelve, too Biblical? All of them were dressed alike, seated, staring wide eyed at the steaming pizza. Father stood. As he did, all the children bow their heads exactly forty-five degrees and close their eyes. Father is mechanic or a farmer. His stubby fingers are stained with grease and his cuticles are black. He was wearing the same suit his dad got married in, powder blue and still out of fashion. He spread his arms, palms up over the feast.

He closed his eyes and gave thanks for all of this, much like Jesus praying over His Pepsi and pepperoni at the last supper. Father thanked everyone from the God-fearing farmer who grew the vegetables to the illegal aliens who hopefully washed their hands before picking those vegetables.

"...and thank you, Lord, for our youngens, who are made in your image. They are white and blond and home-schooled, just like you were before the Jews killed you dead. We are here today to celebrate their birthday which happens to be the same day, except for Caleb, our third twin, who was born after midnight. We eagerly await Armageddon so things can be like the way they were back in the old days."

Everyone said Amen, raised their heads and waited for their slice in silence.

On the other side of the room, at a small round table, two older women sat. Between them on the table is a now empty pizza pan loaded with greasy napkins and a liter carafe now less than half full of Chablis. They were laughing and reminiscing. They stopped now and then to watch Richard, the new bartender, bending over to bus the table down the way. Drinking wine, laughing and reliving the old days, they were truly cute.

Another set of tables was pushed together to accommodate a family. They seemed to be celebrating a young girl's birthday. She was maybe twelve or thirteen. She had long shiny black hair with white ribbons interwoven into braids on both sides of her head. She wore a white dress and was constantly talking to her cousin. They were about the same age and giggled quite a bit with a similar tone and cadence.

The young children in the family ran around the table playing with the free balloons on sticks present at the front door in a brass umbrella holder.

The three men in the family sat next to each other. They were dressed in white shirts and blue jeans with fine tooled Mexican cowboy boots. They laughed out loud, exposing their gold framed teeth which were pointed at by the toothpick they each had in their mouths. They were all happy. They were a family. They were partying with each other and thinking of bonds made and days gone by.

I remember when I was a kid; my grandmother had an electric clock on her kitchen wall. The clock resembled Felix the Cat. It was black and shaped like the lovable cartoon character. Its stomach was the face of the clock with white numerals and hands. It had an "S" shaped tail that swung back and forth. As the tail swung, the eyes of the smiling Felix would articulate back and forth.

We were in the middle of our pizza meal. My wife was scanning the diners and reporting her findings to me. Suddenly she became silent. Her face rose to focus on the incoming diner. At this point she reminded me of my grandmother's clock, not the tail part but the eyes part.

Before she could explain herself I heard someone behind me bellowing, "I saw that! I saw you roll your eyes, young lady!"

I hate it when people stand behind me and start talking about something important to them, and I cannot tell how far they are going to take their rage. You know I can't spin around as fast as I used to back in the old days.

It was even harder to read my wife's face now. In addition to her eyes, now the size of saucers speeding back and forth like a train crossing sign, her mouth fell open to show everyone her food choices. Both hands shot up to cover the cave opening. Each hand held at least four napkins to shield her from onlookers.

"It's perfectly legal! Pierre is a Service Dog! He is here to save my life!"

I still can't figure out what's going on. I tried to twist my head around to see the commotion. Meanwhile the lady moved closer to our table. This could be a good thing or it could be a bad thing. I looked at my wife. She was frozen, eyes flashing, mouth gaping, she was completely speechless.

Then I saw the spectacle. The woman was close to six feet tall. Her large face was red. "My Pierre has never hurt anyone. In fact he saved my life many times! He's a real service dog. I know he doesn't look like a German Shepard but he really is a service dog. I can't say it enough, he's completely harmless. He wouldn't hurt anyone. He saves lives." The words were shot out in rapid fire fashion.

Then I saw Pierre. Pierre was being held by the tall big faced woman. He was a mid-sized poodle with long curly black hair. He was wearing a yellow rain coat, just like that guy on the fish sticks box. Pierre must have left his yellow hat back on the trawler.

Then the saver of lives did that thing all dogs, service or not, do when they get their head wet. He began shaking his head to remove the rain water from his curls. My wife and I fought each other for enough napkins to cover our food before the sprinkler hit the pizza. We both tried to haunch over our food to protect it from the deluge. No use, everything was hosed down. After the storm re-enactment, I removed my glasses to dry them off.

Even though facial expressions are hard to detect on poodles, Pierre looked happy. He seemed to be smiling with his tongue hanging out, panting. Obviously he was hot in his yellow rain coat; it was snapped up all the way to his throat, but I still think he was smiling.

"Pierre wouldn't hurt anyone! He's a service dog!" she repeated again.

Head proudly upright and surveying the restaurant with a steely stare, Pierre now looked noble like a fireman in his yellow turnout coat returning from rescuing an entire family of tall red faced people from a burning pizzeria, quenching the flames on the way out of the building with a snap of the head.

My wife gulps, "I'm-in-a, I'm-in-a, I'm-in-a."

I noticed that the tall big faced woman's tall big faced family had already passed by and were seating themselves two tables behind my wife. They also were in tall big faced disbelief at my wife's obvious lack of enlightenment. They seemed to not understand how my wife could be that old and yet never heard of Pierre the Service Dog. She must be from the Midwest, they must have thought.

Refusing to go sit with her family, she continued with her awkward tribute to her pet. "Just because he doesn't have one of those vests that say he is a service dog, doesn't mean he isn't. He saved my life."

My wife regained her composure and we both mouthed a silent "wow" in unison.

"I have that thing that makes you fall asleep."

"Narcolepsy?" my wife inquired. She was now completely over her shock.

"No, that other thing," the tall big faced lady retorted. "One time, I fell asleep in a movie theater, and Pierre woke me up so I could see the end of the movie. I love him so much! He's like a real person only smarter. Dogs know if you need help even before you do."

I shot a look to my wife that asked her not to encourage her, too late.

"Really?"

Oh, no!

"Oh, yes! I knew you would understand."

What? I said to myself. I suggested we just leave our soggy pizza and go home. As we were leaving, the tall, big faced woman was taking her seat with her family. Pierre was sitting in his place of honor in her big crossed arms. As they settled in, the woman took off his yellow raincoat. He was now wearing his OR scrubs and his little service stethoscope.

On the way to the car, we noticed the rain had stopped. The sun broke through a cloud and caused the rain water to evaporate from the parking lot. The lot steamed and appeared to be the top part of a cloud. We were definitely in a different world, completely different than the one I remembered. We discussed it on the way home.

I understand that service animals fill a very important role in offering an amount of independence to those of us who need it. With that said, I still believe there ought to be a line we should not cross. Where do we stop?

I read about a guy in India who carried a snake with him, in case the man would fall down or lose his footing. His service snake would hold its breath and become stiff so that the man could use him as a cane until he was safe.

Then there was the lady in New Jersey who owned a service parrot that was on hand in case she would lose her voice. The parrot would fly to the neighbor's house to continue gossiping until she regained her voice.

My son says I should get used to it. He says that in Portland, dogs and people work and relax together almost interchangeably. They don't have to make up heroic stories about their pets just to sit with them in public. He says there is a coffee shop in the Pearl District where everyone has a dog with them. If you forget your dog at home or your dog is still working and doesn't get off until seven, you can get a loaner dog to help you with your crossword puzzle, or sometimes you can get the Sudoku service dog. He's very popular and he also works the swing shift as a barista. It's like I once heard, maybe on TV, it's just not like the old days.

My wife said I should get a service monkey to help me type up my stories. She thinks no one could tell the difference.

Chapter Two: A WEEKEND AT HOME

"Spumonium? I don't think that's a real word."

"Oh, it is. It is a newly discovered element. It was discovered in Italy three years ago after a scientist had dinner at the new Olive Garden. I read it in the newspaper."

"What? I've never heard such a thing."

"Oh, yeah. It's too new to be in the dictionary, don't even look. Two triple letters and a triple word, plus fifty points for using all my letters, two hundred forty five points."

"Are you sure?"

"Absolutely, seven, six, two, two, three, eight, ten, fifteen, fifteen that's sixty-five times three plus fifty equals two hundred forty-five."

"No, I mean spumonium. I don't…"

"Too late, I already wrote it down, in ink."

"Oh, man!"

"Look, if you're going to question every word…"

"No, no it's okay. Here, D,O,G, DOG. Happy? Five points." That's why I don't enjoy Scrabble with my wife or as I call it, Squabble. You see, if I would have come up with Spumonium, my wife would have given me that small straight line smile and her head would move from left to right about five eighths of an inch each way.

The straight line smile is something that I believe is hard-wired into all women. Remember Leonardo Da Vinci? He saw this and displayed it to us in the painting of Mona Lisa. Since it was only a painting, he could not show us the head movement, but I'm sure it was there.

"Don't feel so bad, Honey. Tomorrow I'll make you blueberry pancakes."

"You know I'm a pancake whore."

The next morning my wife made blueberry pancakes.

Ahh!

Afterward, I was working on the computer as she cleaned up in the kitchen.

"Is it just me or did the lights blink?"

Just then my desk lamp went from seventy-five to about four and a half watts. It was on, but just barely. 'No, I've got it here too."

We have underground utilities where we live. In the sidewalk next to the garage is an underground vault. I never really knew what was under the grating of the vault; I just knew it went CLUNK, CLUNK as I walked on it.

Last month an electric company worker came to my door to ask me to move my car. At that time we were experiencing an outage, so I felt that if there was anything that I could do to help speed up the down time, I would do it. I moved the car and asked the worker what was going on.

He told me he was the foreman, and he had to look inside our vault to see if the transformer was still working. The outage was limited to our neighborhood, and there were several transformers that he had to check. Our transformer must have been okay, because I looked outside ten minutes later and the foreman was gone.

Three hours later the power was back on. The transformer up the street was replaced, and except for the power surge that took out my television, all was good. A couple times during the following weeks, I could smell an odor similar to burning. I passed it off as just the neighbor kids smoking dope.

So, as the light bulb dimmed at my desk, the light bulb over my head got brighter. They changed at the same rate going in different directions. The light bulbs met each other in the middle. At that time they were at the same intensity, I figured it out.

I walked over to the front door, opened it and looked outside. Billowing from the grate over the vault was thick black smoke. The neighbor kids were now exonerated.

I called the fire department and explained the story to the captain when he arrived. By now the smoke was white and not so billowy. The captain told me he had called the electrical company. I had to move the car again, this time for the fire truck. The fire crew arrived and took turns looking down at the grate.

I know the fire crew was disappointed they couldn't chop holes in my newly shingled roof. They had to leave all that porn back at the station and could only stand there looking down at the grate and then up at the roof, swallow then grimace. The captain stayed for an hour, waiting to tell the electric company foreman his version of what happened. The fire crew went back to the firehouse, not letting all that porn go to waste.

I met with the electrical foreman outside after I saw the fire captain drive away. No use letting all that...you know.

The foreman looked down and kicked some of the leaves away from the vault. His crew showed up in two different rigs, a big one with a cherry picker and a pick-up with signs and barriers. The foreman said he would know more when they opened up the vault. They seemed to be still assembling so I went back inside.

It was starting to cool off a bit in the house as I went back to my crossword. It was after one o'clock, but with no lights on inside the house and January on the outside it appeared much later. The thermostat kept reminding me how cold it actually was. It would drop a degree about every twenty minutes. My wife reminded me that if I quit looking out the door, the house would stay warmer. I turned around and saw that straight line smile. I closed the door and went back to my desk without looking for the head movement.

After the temperature dropped another degree, I went outside to check on the crew. There were more people from the electric company than the fire department and I knew why. The fire department is a volunteer organization and it was Sunday so the electric company is paying double time.

Instead of taking turns looking at the grate like the firemen, the electricians gathered around the vault as the apprentice opened the hinged grated top. One of the workers said for someone to go to the truck to get a shovel to hold the top from falling all the way down. Nobody moved. The foreman focused his eyes on the man leaning against the wall of the garage.

"Hey, man, don't look at me! I'm the flagger." He then pointed to the dirty safety cone sitting on the curb. His apprentice nodded in agreement.

Someone, probably the electrical apprentice, handed the foreman a shovel. Three of the electricians propped the lid with the shovel. Now they all could peer into the vault. The vault had long since stopped smoking. They sprang into action. Two journeymen handed fiberglass poles to the two apprentices next to the hole. They started poking around with these orange poles. It reminded me of when I worked. We would have the apprentices hand the tools to us as we worked, except of course on Sunday. You know, double time.

I asked, "I know you guys are just starting, but do you have an estimate on how long this might take?"

The flagger, still resting his butt on my garage, shook his head and rubbed his stubby chin.

The foreman said, "We're going to have to dump the neighborhood."

"Does that mean we have to leave?"

"Eh, whatever you want."

Hmm.

I went back inside and gave them another fifteen minutes and one more degree. This time when I went outside, the foreman was not around. I raised my eyebrows to the worker.

He said, "About two more hours."

The flagger nodded.

"Okay." I went inside.

My wife raised her eyebrows to me.

I pursed my lips, looked up and said, "Two more hours, ma'am." Then I nodded.

"What's taking so long?"

"Well, it's Sunday and the new parts are hard to come by. You should know, there're made of Spumonium. Let's go for lunch and warm up."

I was given a straight line smile and left-right movement.

Chapter Three: MY OLD BAR

"Mommy, what's a skank?" The cute little red haired moppet inquired. "That lady said skank. What's a skank? Is it like a skunk? Like on Bambi? Skank! Skank! Skank! Hee Hee Hee! I'm not a skank, I'm a skunk, like Flower!"

Kids are smarter than they get credit for. I could have sat there for hours before I came up with "Flower." That's why I like watching kids in their environment, and three year olds are by far the cutest and funniest. Art Linkletter was right; kids do say the darnedest things.

But, wait a minute, I'm not in a day care or a kindergarten or even a family reunion. This isn't their environment, this is mine, or at least I thought it was. It was only two months ago when this was a neighborhood/biker bar. Today it's a neighborhood/family bar where kids can accompany their parents until nine PM at which time it converts back to a neighborhood biker bar with the same old crowd as before.

I don't know if it's a new law or maybe they made a deal with the old crowd allowing them time to watch *Wheel of Fortune* and wipe the thirty-weight off the kitchen table after working on the drive chain, but that's the way it is now days. It's still a bar, but I think the crossover time could be kind of tricky.

The source of today's new vocabulary word now becomes evident. Ironically, she shared the same hair color as the little tyke, but I'm pretty certain the three year old is wearing her original hue. On three year old girls I think the color might be called: OH MY GOD, SHE'S IRISH RED and this curly bob was touched off with a cute green bow.

On the forty-five year old, the same color looks a little brassier and comes with a warning from Revlon or Krylon regarding open flames. The same bow looks a bit washed out and perched on top of the tumble weed, it is pretty hard to see.

"So I told that skank, 'You stay away from my Bobby or I'll cut you open, you dirty skank!' She acted like I was the one on crack. So I gave her the old snake eye and then she knew better. That dirty skank! I don't care if her old man is a minister!" This was followed by a hoarse laugh, oxygen seeking gasp and a lung emptying series of coughs. Instinctively my eyes lowered, not out of respect; I was looking for things to bounce off the floor: spittle, small organs or maybe her socks. Nothing.

The whole buddy bar roared as Brenda bent over convulsing. It was quite a sight, Brenda's red face pointing to the floor and her butt sticking up in the air. Her shirt pulled up on her back, and her low-rider jeans pulled down enough to expose her lower back tattoo, NO PARKING in two and a half inch red capital letters with a matching red arrow pointing down the crack of her butt. Her knees buckled as she grabbed on the bar stool with her left hand and steadied herself enough to stand semi-erect. The crowd roared again. She rose to her toes with her arms up, hands pointing out much like a much older Nadia Comaneci. She tried to cough out a TA DA, but had to settle for only half, "DA." Beer spilled all around the buddy bar as Brenda righted herself finally. Wiping spittle from her mouth, her head bobbed up and down as she regained her focus. "Bobby! Get me another Jaeger!"

The guy at the end of the bar in the sleeveless plaid shirt snapped his head up as he heard his name. His shiny black hair was slicked back and he had a

Camel straight behind his left ear. I figured it was there in case he was challenged to a speed light up competition. He quickly removed his right hand from the back pocket of the tight Levis next to him. A disappointed scowl replaced the soothing smile on the blond next to Bobby.

"Honey!" Bobby called out to the bartender, "My Brenda needs another Jaeger."

When the bartender looked up to acknowledge his order, Bobby held up two fingers just above the bar then pointed down with his index finger and moved it side to side in front of his big belt buckle. The bartender nodded knowingly. Bobby mouths the words, "I owe you, baby."

Another nod.

The bartender went back to the other end of the bar to chase a twelve year old away from the Test Your Love machine after he deposited his quarter.

"I'm sorry, Sugar! You gotta get down off that bar stool. It's the law. You gotta stay six feet away from the bar in case one of these old cowboys would tip over. You don't want them to land on your head, do ya?

I saw a two year old waddle toward LeRoy Jr.'s pit bull, Spike. LeRoy and Spike sat in their usual stool three away from the juke box. The little boy had a partially clean rib bone in his hand. He waved it over his head as he waddled toward the dog. Spike smiled.

Another round of laughter arose as Brenda gulped her Jaeger and wiped her mouth with her sweaty arm.

"See, Mommy, they're laughing. Skank. Skank. Skank."

I looked at the face of the mother. Her brow was knitted as she stared at her husband then she smiled. I realized she wasn't even listening to the child. They were making plans for the weekend.

Then it hit me. What was I worried about? These aren't my kids. Maybe, this is just a time saving device. If you think about it, when was the last time you saw old Uncle Bert bouncing a nephew on his knee at a family gathering? It wasn't because we were running out of young nephews to molest. Uncle Bert just doesn't show up any more. Who needs him? Now there is Ernie 'five hundred feet' Williams. Ernie shows up every other day or so at the neighborhood bar. So who needs Uncle Bert when Ernie just lives down the street? You don't have to find him lodging or help clean up after he leaves.

Yuk!

Remember Brenda? You know it's not much of a stretch to think how Brenda and your cousin Paula are very much alike. How can you forget the stories of her colorful antics? Like the time cousin Paula stripped down to her underpants and began singing a funny song, which ended with her holding up her naked breasts at the family picnic. Grandma was chasing her around with a beach towel, trying to cover up her indignities. Too late! We haven't seen her for a while either, come to think of it.

My point is, everyone with a family has somebody with a very similar personality of the customers that show up at the neighborhood bar. At the bar, the kids are exposed to and can learn from all sorts of topics: politics, religion, political religion and religious politics. Also on tap: minorities, sex, sexual minorities and sex with minorities. It could be educational.

You might as well be allowed to bring the kids down to the bar; after all, for the most part, the kids might not even be here if it weren't for the bar. It might also act as a sobering up moment for those who might be thinking about saving a little money on contraception tonight. Besides, you might just hear:

"Mommy, what's a blow job? Blow Job, Blow Job, Blow Job. Hee Hee Hee."

Chapter Four: DRINKING COFFEE IN PORTLAND

We were in the Pearl District of Portland. My wife and I found a table on the sidewalk in the shade of a maple tree. She had her cappuccino and I had my black coffee with a double shot. Everywhere you go they have a different name for my choice; Shot in the Dark, Depth Charge, Terminator, Pile Driver. Here they call it The Buzz Master. I always order them by describing it to the barista, the baristas always look above my head as if they are reading the side of a blimp, blink once for each ingredient named, smile then ask, "Do you mean a ___?"

"Why, yes I do!"

At the table next to us are two guys in their early twenties. They are wearing faded black tee shirts, black holy jeans with silver studded belts set to forty inches on their thirty inch waists, a chain connected to their wallet, striped boxers only showing eight above the top of their jeans and a pair of Vans. They almost look identical except for the irony in the fact that the one with green shoes had spiky yellow hair and the one with yellow shoes had spiky green hair. I gathered that one was named Man and the other was named Dude.

I swear it went exactly like this:

"I got cloudcoma, man. I need some medication so I can see straight. I got my medical card in Albuquerque, and you know how hard it is to get a card down there. It's not like California. You can get one in a Wheaties box in Modesto. I got this eye condition so I got my card."

"You've got an eye condition, dude?

"Yeah, I can't see myself without any smoke. Ha Ha Ha! So now you're telling me just because I laminated my card, I can't use it here?"

"That's right, dude!"

"Well that's just shit! You got a fucked-up state here, man. You'll see what happens when go down to New Mexico. I'm going to tell all my friends, you'll be dead to them. You won't be able to buy a pack of Zigzags."

"Chill, Spud! I didn't say I couldn't help you. It'll just take some situating."

"You can do that from here?"

"Same as. Just go two blocks that way; in the middle of the block is Needle Nose Tattoo and Piercing. That's where I got my snake tattoo, check it out. Any ways, next door to that is a stairway going up to my doctor's office. Old Doc Green will fix you up. He'll fix your clowncoma for half the price of those fuckin' hippy doctors."

"Wait, I don't want it fixed, man. I just need my medication."

"That's what I mean Bone Head. He'll write you an Oregon prescription. Boy, you new Mexicans sure are simple. Did you ride your board all the way to Portland? Don't you know those diesel fumes can soften your brain?"

"No, I took the bus, fucker."

"I know you are a blond white dude but what else does it take to be a new Mexican?

"I'm not a new Mexican. I'm a New Mexican. It's a fuckin' state, man!"

"I know. I'm just fuckin' with ya." Heh Heh! He's a new Mexican. Heh Heh! Hey, what do you call a Mexican in a dress?"

"I don't know. What?"

"Senorita! Ha Ha Ha! Get it? Senorita!"

"Yeah, I get it. So any way, if I see your guy, he'll only cost me fitty dollars?"

"No, Moron! Fifty! Fifty! Fifffty!! Remember where you are dude! Show some dignity. Fuck! You know if you act like a hillbilly, they'll ask you for all kinds of ID then you're sunk, since all you have is that New Mexican stuff. You know you can't spend those new pesos up here."

"We use dollars in Albuquerque, how many times do I…"

"Hey, come on, man, let's go. We'll go see my guy."

After the exchange, they rose from their chairs. They clasped each other's right arms at the wrists, like the Lone Ranger and Tonto congratulating each other after their plan worked out and they caught the bad guys. I could visualize a bad guy somewhere fanning his hand up and down like he's playing an invisible ukulele after having it slapped with a silver bullet.

We never did learn their names, but we didn't care. The boys were completely precious, but it was good to see them go away. I wanted more coffee ten minutes ago, but I didn't want to leave for a second.

"This is why I like taking you for coffee in Portland, Baby."

Chapter Five: ONE DAY IN ST. LOUIS

Last summer, while in vacation, we found ourselves waiting for a train in St. Louis, MO. We couldn't get a later checkout time from our room, so we decided we could spend the time hanging out at the train station.

One thing we did discovered traveling by train was that America has some beautiful gems hidden inside its older, grander, historic cities. These gems are the train stations that are located in the older, grander, historic parts of these cities.

As Western America grew, it grew from the train stations out. The railroad stitched its way west across the country, and at necessary intervals it built stations to refuel and take on the ever growing ridership that it served. In the early days of the twentieth century, the railroad companies were the largest companies in America, larger than some counties and kingdoms in Europe. As a show of their wealth and power, they built functional monuments of their greatness. The station became a showplace of their opulence. Stone walls, grand arches, marble floors and large spaces to hold the modern travelers in awe as well as in safety.

As train travel decreased, due to the automobile and air travel, the station became almost forgotten and ignored. Soon many of them were in the less attractive parts of these older cities. Thankfully, during the latter part of the twentieth century, the cities began revitalizing the older more historic downtown areas. Many cities have polished their gems and the settings that hold them. Restaurants and shops are dressed up in matching brick and stone. Old style street lamps lead the way through pedestrian walkways, taxi lanes and bus routes that once held fast moving automotive traffic. The cities realize that, in many cases, the station was their mother, and they want to pay homage to her. And then there is St. Louis.

St. Louis has spent millions on her mother, only her mother is the riverfront area of the Mississippi. Beautiful parks and shops line the slow moving, nerve soothing downtown area of St. Louis. No iconic stone fronted symbol of the day of the train for St. Louis. Perched over the tracks of forgotten ages, access to St. Louis Station is a winding ramp with a small parking lot at the top.

Stone and brick are not the materials used here, instead aluminum and glass, just like we used to build our modern malls in the sixties. Art Deco gives way to Art Neglecto. Robins' egg blue glass and ceramic tile line the inside of the dual use room. No hand carved pews for the seating area. Pews are replaced by stainless steel and fiberglass chairs bolted to the concrete floor. At the end of each row you will find an aluminum ashtray with a piece of metal pop riveted to the top of it in order to send you outside to burn one. Under the tray is a trash can that can be accessed from the front and side only.

Remember back in the third grade when you had to share your room with a sibling for a week while relatives stayed at your house on their vacation? In St. Louis, Amtrak has to share her room with her little sister, Greyhound. Not for a week but forever.

The bickering sisters are on either side of the open seating area. Each use nylon crowd control straps dispensed from stainless steel stanchions to keep their own crowds controlled in front of their own identical ticket/information counter. Even though they tried to dress differently, Mom made them semi matching uniforms.

We found it easy to detect the 'Snake-Eye' being shot across the room at each other from time to time when they thought no one was looking. If you had a question when you arrived and mistakenly went to the wrong unmarked ticket/information counter, the lady would smile and whisper that you have to go to the other side. You apologize for not seeing the invisible sign. As you turn to see the length of the line on the other side, you decided your question wasn't that important anyway. As you leave, you see the Greyhound lady take something out of her smock pocket, turn and appear to stab it repeatedly with a letter opener, hit it with a stapler three times and put it back in her pocket. She then spins around with her caring smile and whispers to the next questioner.

Since we got here a bit early, it was time to find something to eat. I decided to go outside to find a restaurant. I forgot where we were; St. Louis, mid-July, afternoon.

I have transitional lenses in my glasses, you know, the kind that gets you accustomed to the sunlight automatically. I wished someone had invented transitional clothing, you know, the kind that falls off automatically when you are immediately exposed to one hundred and ten degree heat complemented with one hundred and ten percent humidity.

Impossible, you say?

No!

I gasped for air, removed my transitional glasses to dry off my lenses and covered my squinting, sweating eyes from the bright July sunshine. Not seeing where I was going, I walked into several people. I coughed out an, "I am sorry; I can't see were I'm going. Oh yes, that is my shirt, thank you." I walked out the East exit all the way around to the South entrance, the short way. I walked back into the 'stationette', adjusting my glasses and tucking in my shirt.

My discovery expedition yielded only the fact that we alone on top of this artificial hillside. As I re-entered, I asked one of my toothless fellow travelers where she got that food she seemed to be enjoying. Thankfully, she only pointed behind herself as she gulped more food. Down to the left was an alcove.

Inside it and to the right was a counter. Behind the counter was a young girl. The girl's uniform matched the theme of the restaurant; it was a Chicken-Bell-Hut. I ordered pizza.

We ate over our luggage. Our bags were right in front of us because in order to carry our suitcases to the train, we had to keep them with us. There is no storage between here and the train. We ate our food and slid our refuse into the slot below the former ashtray.

While we were waiting in the waiting area, we were entertained by the best St. Louis and the entire Mid-West could provide. No one could understand a syllable being projected over the public address system. From where we sat, it seemed the microphones were a hybrid between a tomato soup can and a kazoo.

When there was an important announcement to be made by Amtrak or Little Greyhound, it would be preceded by a short blast of static from the speaker system. For some reason one sister would begin her important message just before her sister's message would stop reverberating across the room. People, who thought they could glean information from the echoing din, would cock their head to one side, look up and close one eye in hopes to zero in on the needed information. Acoustical depth perception was impossible to establish in this building. It was hard to tell if you were hearing the baby in front of you crying or the kid behind you. Everything echoed and mixed together to make an audio soup that no one liked or understood.

Travelers flowed in and out of the station. The majority were bus riders. After the lead bus traveler deduced which sister to talk to, the rest of the bus riders would stand in that line with their portable possessions for their turn to whisper. Train riders slowly grew in number, all of us waiting for the time to walk down that long gangway that led to down stairs and the tracks.

The 'trainers' seemed to like watching the 'bussers' try to cope in the strange environment, and with a new bus arriving every twenty minutes, the show never ended. We would all watch the bus people file in, make connections or be greeted by loved ones and move on. We had time to kill and the real life theater-in-the-round, put on for free, made time go by quickly. Then the time slowed way down. Train riders still had at least twenty five minutes before our call to board but it might as well have been twenty five years, considering what happened next.

Urgency replaced complacency. High voltage electricity crackled all around us like the report of a twenty-two foot bull whip. It silenced the insufficient PA system. They came from somewhere in Georgia or Alabama, and we weren't at all ready for this. With almost all of the train riders in their fiberglass seats, only three chairs were vacant in the building. They were directly in front of me and my wife, eight feet away, facing us. Train riding loved ones grasped each other's hands. Heads bowed down except for the one eye that stayed focused on the spectacle. We tried to look somewhere else, but we were all transfixed. No one spoke, no one moved, no one dared.

In they flew; mother, father and two small girls. The girls were about two and one years old. They were silent but their posture showed they would rather be anyplace but here. Mom was talking to all three of them separately but at the same time at the top of her lungs. They all cowered silently, as did we. Sweat was squirting from mom's forehead like a Rain Bird, followed by the staccato of spittle and words that were pushed through her gap toothed grill. The older daughter carried her own Strawberry Shortcake backpack. The baby was carried by mom along with a backpack while tugging a wheeled suitcase that seemed to keep rolling over on its side every three steps. This only made her sputter more. Dad carried the rest of the gear, keeping his eyes pointed down. His head would bend lower with each word intended for him.

"I can't understand why they canceled our bus! Now we only have ten minutes to catch our next bus!" I'm sure this was meant for dad.

It was meant for dad, but one hundred and ten train goers now understand more and you could hear a collective, "Hmmm."

"Go in there and get this straightened out right now, Dewayne!" She made it sound like his name was spelled with all capital letters. She wore a white baggy tee shirt that hung to her knees. A white athletic shirt, under that, could be seen through the arm holes. She wore tight white knee length stretch pants and flip-flops. Hair colored straw was stacked on top her head and held in place somehow using several different devices: a clip, a chopstick, a sixteen penny nail and a pair of brass knuckles. You may think I was exaggerating but I wasn't. It was 'hair colored straw'.

The baby was being carried much like the mother orangutan carried her baby on the Discovery Channel. The baby's extra-long arms were draped over mom's arm. Although the baby had thin white hair and not orange, I still felt compelled to give her a banana.

Mom laid the baby down in the middle chair, right in front of us and quickly changed her diaper. I started to wonder how many kids had their pants changed on my chair before I got there. Yeeuck! She then sat Little Sister in the middle chair wedged her in place with Big Sister's backpack. A half bag of chips were dumped on a suitcase in front of Big Sister. "Here, honey, eat your snack", as she fashioned the now empty chip bag into a makeshift fan to cool her neck.

Dewayne wore a white tee shirt, black jeans and white athletic shoes. The Greyhound terminal manager's office was next to the ticket/information counter. His sweaty blond head shook as he tried to explain to her that he hadn't had a cigarette in four hours. When she wouldn't listen to him, he dropped his head and tried to explain it to his shoes. Someone had to listen to him. His empty hands shook as he dragged himself to the office.

He vanished into the office. Several minutes later, shouting escaped out of the closed door and boomed over the awkward silence. One hundred and ten eaves droppers strained to understand the conversation, but to no avail. The young man bolted out of the office. The shaky hands were cradling his forehead as it swayed back and forth in disbelief and dread. Now he had to face her. We all knew he had bad news to deliver. We hushed completely.

"Did you tell him we have to get there for my daddy's funeral? Did you tell him we are going to be late? What do you mean, you need a cigarette? You have to take care of this, Dewayne!"

"He said he would call security if I didn't leave his office," Dewayne tried to whisper. "I can't have that happen. I just got out of prison. I don't even have any ID."

One hundred and ten silent "Oohs."

"Well I haven't had a cigarette either, Dewayne! Why are you always just thinking about yourself? You wait here with the babies, and I'll have a cigarette then it's your turn." She stormed out.

Fifty five "Murmur murmurs." Followed by fifty five "Murmur, murmur, murmurs."

Four and a half minutes later, Mom returned. "Now it's your turn, Dewayne, and hurry back, I have to take Baby to the bathroom!"

When I was a kid, one of my favorite comic characters was a dummy. I mean a real dummy. His name was Jerry Mahoney. He used to work with Paul Winchell. They worked together telling jokes and thrilling millions of kids. Paul was the straight man. The straight man delivers the set-up lines for the comic who adds the zinger and then usually a funny face of disbelief. Jerry was famous for his jaw drop and eye shift.

The jaw drop was always funny. Jerry's mouth dropped open and made a "snap" sound. As a kid I used to practice this all day. The eye shift was even funnier than the jaw drop. Jerry could move both of his eyes at the same time to the left or the right. Jerry usually moved his eyes to the right. He would do this after Paul said something stupid. The eye shift was accompanied by a "click" sound. The jaw drop and the eye shift are both called "takes." Whenever Jerry used a "take," we would laugh our guts out.

Two and a half minutes later, Dewayne returned from his smoke break. Out of breath from running back inside, his now steady hands were combing back his wet blond hair. He guarded Little Sister while Mom took Big Sister to the restroom. When the girls returned, things started back up just like someone had removed a giant bookmark. Mom arrived, already in mid-sentence.

"...tell him my daddy was dead, Dewayne? Did you tell him we've been riding the bus for three days? Did you tell him we are going to be late and my daddy is going to be buried tomorrow and I haven't seen his poor dead body? I haven't said good-bye yet! Dewayne, I was depending on you to do your part and what do you do? You go in there and pick a fight with the manager. Now we can't get any help to get home and see my daddy! What were you thinking, Dewayne? Now I got to get back to the bathroom and you got to watch the kids 'til I'm back!"

"But, honey."

"Don't talk back to me, Dewayne! Don't you know I'M HAVING MY PERIOD RIGHT HERE IN PUBLIC!"

St. Louis: mid-July, one hundred and ten degrees, one hundred and ten percent humidity, one hundred and ten "Snaps," one hundred and ten "Clicks."

Chapter Six: THE ZABADABAS

The Mexican state of Nayarit holds some of the most picturesque and spacious beaches in Mexico. Alongside these beaches are the quaintest villages you will ever encounter. Travel north from the Puerto Vallarta airport just forty miles and sixty years and you will discover six or seven small oceanfront hamlets.

From these fishing villages, the local fishermen still launch their small colorful boats from the beach, return with their catch and sell their morning work to the giant hotels that dot the coastline. By noon, the men return to relax in the shade of the palm trees that separate the white beaches from the green mountainous jungle.

My favorite of these villages is the small town of San Francisco, or as the locals call it, San Pancho. Pancho is the diminutive form of Francisco. A mile west of Highway 2 by way of a bumpy dirt road hides this gem that is both modern and ancient. During the early seventies, the President of Mexico made San Pancho a pet project of his. A state-of-the-art hospital was built on the hill above the town. He also constructed schools, streets, sewers and a water purification system to make every drop of water in San Pancho potable and refreshing.

This was his favorite resort area and he wanted it to become a tourist destination. During his administration, he visited San Panache frequently as both president and 'first tourist'. A presidential term does not last forever, even in Mexico. When a new president was elected, he had his own favorite place; it wasn't San Pancho.

The pueblo aged and not all of the president's changes took root. The hospital, schools and water system still exist, but the streets are a checkerboard of cobblestone and dirt. The several hundred people that call San Pancho home quietly go about their business fishing or working in nearby resorts. The pineapple cannery on the main street into San Pancho, which has long since closed down, may help distract the nosy tourist from venturing further. Its remaining walls look more like a bombed out structure in a war torn part of the world. A small store, a couple small cantinas and three restaurants all dot the four blocks that are the downtown of San Pancho. One block north will find the school and church. At the end of the main street is a small parking lot, cantina, white sand and the Pacific Ocean.

Half way through town, next to a vacant building, is a small sky blue sign with white lettering that says one mile north to Olla Azul —Blue Wave. Travel this one lane dirt road with its taxi swallowing pot holes exactly one mile and you will encounter Olla Azul Hotel and Restaurant. Olla Azul is promoted as a sports resort.

They have available: SCUBA diving, snorkeling, kayaking, hiking and mountain biking in the jungle. When they say available, they mean they will take you by van to these destinations at nine in the morning and bring you back at five. When the sports minded are out for the day, the resort is all but vacant. Those who are left behind have the place to themselves.

The hotel has twelve units with a pool view and six units two blocks away on the other side of the dirt road tucked away in the jungle. We started out in one of those jungle units, but the refrigerator door rusted itself off the hinges in

1984 and kept falling off every time you opened it. We complained and got a unit next to the pool.

We spent the following week doing absolutely nothing. Up at ten, breakfast, lie by the pool until lunch. Lunch is on the deck just off the large open aired palapa that is the restaurant and bar. Eat shrimp in the hot sun with a cool ocean breeze and use two or three Pacificos to wash them down. Back to the pool for an hour and a half until it is time to take a nap. Cocktails, then dine at seven.

After dinner, the Olla Azul restaurant would put on a production of some kind because they knew there wasn't much to do in this isolated place after dark. If you had rented a car to get there, you would think twice about going away for the evening to another resort for a couple drinks only to drive the snaky Highway 2 through the jungle in the dark. Therefore all eighteen units were available to watch the nightly special. One night was tequila tasting, one night was a fourteen piece Mariachi band and one night was a night on the beach, traveling in the dark down the coast to see the hatching of the turtle eggs. I say "see" but it's really not "see" the hatching in the dark with only the moonlight to guide you; flashlights were forbidden.

Tonight was different. Tonight there was a special guest with a special presentation. The presentation was crafted to fit the sports minded, green obliged, sandal wearing crowd that surrounded us. The median age of our dinner mates was probably thirty one. My wife and I brought my son Matt. Matt was nineteen and on break from college. Matt helped bring down our age average.

We sat along the north wall of the palapa trying to capture any ocean breeze that might be out there that night. It was pretty still in the palapa. The palm woven blades of the overhead fans grunted as they tried to find enough cool air to deliver down to the sweaty observers of the night's presentation. A special commotion was brewing on the stage area as the demonstration was about to begin.

Miguel, our special waiter, was filling our requests in anticipation of the special presentation.

The lights dimmed. A CD of native music filled the warm jungle air. Flutes with small drums tapping out a foreign but somehow familiar rhythm tried to fill the big room. Its open sides and twenty five foot ceiling let most of the music escape. Those in the back, to my right, who strained to hear anything, moved their chairs closer to save their hearing for tomorrow's sporting event. They complained how their muscles hurt from today's sporting event. After some shushing, the spectators realized a man was speaking up front. Miguel ran from the stage area to the kitchen. A loud crackle, an electronic squeal and the hotel manager/emcee was amplified in mid-sentence, ".....of Nebraska. So please, welcome the Professor.

—Polite applause — More sore muscles.

"Thank you, Sr. Lucas." None of us knew the manager's name, so we murmured. "How many of you watch *Sixty Minutes*?

Everyone raised their right hand. I thought I was back in sixth grade. I knew we were in Mexico, but it seemed like we all just pledged allegiance to *Sixty Minutes*.

The Professor gave a knowing nod. The special presentation had begun. Due to the short in the speaker system, no one really heard the Professor's name. The Professor was about forty, dressed in khaki shorts and safari shirt with long tan knee high socks and hiking boots. I noticed on the table to his right sat a pith helmet, some photographs and a stack of CDs. Sitting at the table, facing the crowd was a very plain white woman. Her eyes were glued on the Professor.

"Did you watch *Sixty Minutes* November fourteenth of last year?" This confused the crowd; some nodded yes, some mouthed the word yes and some raised their right hand again. Thinking it might be a trick question, I closed my eyes trying to remember if I had actually seen that episode. I wanted to be truthful. He continued, "Then you saw the report on The People Time Forgot.

A giant, silent question mark hung over the crowd.

"Maybe you were out that night." He faced raised eyebrows and eyes lifted up to the right. "That's okay! It was also in *Newsweek* the next week."

Thirty eight to forty face saving, "Oh yeah!" lies filled the room. The Professor smiled.

The hook was set.

We didn't realize Miguel wore so many hats. Special bartender, sound technician and now he's stage manager. He was turning off the stage lights except for the baby spot on the Professor and running over to turn on a slide projector and focusing it on the screen behind the Professor.

The image slowly coming into view was a beach next to a jungle. Brown sand on the left side of the image, a small campfire in the middle of the beach and to the right was a jungle scape. The white object in the upper right hand corner was morphing into the *Sixty Minutes* stop watch. Guilt filled the room. A mechanical sound foretold the display of another slide on the screen. This time it was the same photograph with the front cover of *Newsweek* superimposed over the photo.

Wait a minute.

I looked around the room to see everyone looking even guiltier than before. Maybe because where I was seated, on the north wall, I began to see things at a different angle than the crowd, much differently, more than the ninety degrees different.

I was cautious but I didn't know why, yet. I began paying closer attention to the skinny man with the ginger hair and beard.

On with the show:

"I knew you heard about the Zabadabas, I could tell." Everyone puffed up knowing they got away with a white lie.

"Getting away with a lie makes you vulnerable to others more powerful." I once read that on a note in a fortune cookie. So did the Professor.

"I can't tell you where this place is, but it's somewhere in Latin America."

The next slide was the same shot without overlays.

"This is the way to the village of the Zabadabas."

Another photo, this time the interior of a sky blue and white wooden canoe. It was half canoe, half river or lake or maybe even swimming pool.

"You have to travel up stream on a large jungle river until you come to an undiscovered lake tucked into the jungle. At the far end of the lake is the village that I only heard whispers of for twelve years. A village so sacred to the people of the river that it had no name. They only referred to them as Los Viejos or The Ancient Ones. Twelve years of making myself more trustworthy to the river people finally got me permission to meet Los Viejos."

The next photo was of a small brown man stripped to the waist. He had two white stripes on each cheek and a sky blue stripe across his forehead. He had a Moe Howard hair cut with a small arrow through his hair. A thin leather strap over his shoulder supported a small leather pouch. He was standing in his own canoe, the canoe we were introduced to in the previous picture. At his feet was a flour sack with a string near the top keeping it closed. Maybe it was just me but shapes I could detect inside the flour sack seemed to be: a bottle of whiskey, a can of Spam and one of those large eggs that pantyhose came in. The little man was pointing with his right hand to his left. In his left hand he held a small bow.

"I had to promise to never tell the world where they lived. I had a guide take me to where a small stream fed into the big river."

This slide showed a small stream converging with a larger river. Tied to a mangrove tree was a small sky blue sign with two white letters and an arrow pointing to the right. Capital "L" above a capital "V".

Hmm.

Amazon Moe —not his real name —was pointing to the sign.

"It took two days of rowing our canoe to get to the far end of this long lake."

At this time the flute and drum music got louder. It wasn't spooky music, but I saw several couples clutching each other. The next slide was again the first slide. This time at the far right of the photo you could see a bare leg in an action pose as though it were running off the beach and the photograph. A woman in the back shrieked. The Professor smiled.

"My guide dropped me off and promised to return in one week. I was on my own, in the jungle with an unknown people."

I heard someone in the back say in a stage whisper, "No, he didn't die! That's him up there. Jesus, Lori! Pay attention!"

The next slide was the same beach scene with the campfire. This time next to the campfire was a small green nylon tent. Next to the tent were three more flour sacks of goods.

"I decided to camp on the beach to allow them to come to me. They would feel less threatened this way. It didn't take long for me to be discovered. On the morning of the second day on the beach, I woke up with the feeling that I wasn't alone. I peeked out of my tent to see three small brown men poking through my belongings. These men were thin, dressed only in a loin cloth and carried large war axes. These war axes appeared to be Pre-Columbian. I had only seen sketches of similar styled axes in museums. The men were startled by my head popping out of my tent. One man ran to the edge of the jungle, turned and hid behind a large fern. In a blink he was gone, swallowed by the jungle. The other two men looked at each other and then back at me. They began talking to each other. I speak seven languages and at least twelve river dialects. I had never heard a language like this one before. Their language seemed to consist of different pitched clicks, whistles and blinks. I wanted to take their picture, but my camera was outside with my supplies."

No slide change at this time.

Hmm.

With the crowd literally on the edge of their seat, the Professor took a dramatic pause then continued. "I began crawling out of my tent, very slowly, keeping eye contact with the remaining discovery force. They both took two steps backward and then two more steps backward when they realized how tall I was. They were silent now, watching my deliberately slow movements. Their dark eyes were as big as coconuts. One man hefted his ax slightly. It was an impulse. When I was out completely, I sat in front of my tent. I was afraid if I stood up I would scare them off. A whistle and click came from a man just inside the jungle. He was also dressed in a loincloth. He had pure white hair held back with a leather band. He was thin and carried a spear that he used as a walking stick to help support his frail body. Behind him two young girls tried to hide from view. He was too small to shield anyone, and they were too curious to stay out of eye shot. The girls could not have been more than sixteen and wore only a loincloth."

Wooden chair legs screeched on the marble floor after hearing this.

"Maybe, only fourteen"

That did it, everybody was paying attention now, even Miguel.

"The little man began to speak. After a few sentences, he realized I did not understand his message. I tried to understand. It seemed he was gifting me with these two young girls."

Hushed murmurs filled the gallery. The temperature rose dramatically in the palapa.

"I offered him one of my pre-packed goodwill bundles. He bowed and clicked something. I bowed back and mimicked the click. He smiled and offered me his hand. I slowly rose to my feet. On seeing that I was over six feet tall, the warriors began clicking and popping uncontrollably. The old man gave two high pitched whistles and the two men were silent. We bowed to each other again. I reached down and grabbed my day pack. The old man walked into the jungle and I followed. Behind me were the two guards then the girls."

His camera must have been in his day pack because the next slide was that of a small grass hut with a campfire in front of it. Next to the fire was a wooden rack with several fish fillets drying by the fire and the sun. Several paths radiated out from this hut.

"He put the goodwill bundle into the hut and clicked directions to someone inside. We sat next to his fire, and he began to teach me his language. Using hand motions and pantomimes, he was determined to tell his story. Theirs is strictly a verbal language. He did draw in the dirt with a stick on special occasions. He had his people feed us dried fish and wild banana. At the end of the day, he took me down a path and showed me a small hut, just a little larger than my tent. He motioned for me to enter with a smile. I clicked thank you to him, and it wasn't until after he left, that I discovered the two girls from the beach were already in my hut."

Miguel was wiping his brow with his bar towel.

"We spent three days learning a common language. It was a mixture of theirs and a river dialect that I'm sure he learned trading with the few visitors he encountered. He said their people were called the Zabadabas and he was their shaman, Zobo. I told him my name was Gregory."

Gregory?

"He told me his people called me Pleeko-Minko. Drawing in the dirt, he showed me this meant lake turtle that walks outside his shell. This is how I appeared on our first encounter. They thought my clothes were part of my body and my tent was my shell. Lucky for me, the turtle is a sacred omen."

Professor Gregory stopped and sipped from a water bottle. Replacing the cap, he clicked the remote control. The next image was that of Zobo standing in front of his hut, I guess. The little brown man was holding his shaman staff. Somehow, fastened to his loin cloth was a knife. The metal bladed knife more than likely was traded to him by some earlier visitor.

"I asked him to send a messenger back to the lake and give the canoe guide a note that assured him I was safe and to please return in one week. This gave us more time to debrief each other. I found out that their history was very old. They have lived in the same place for nine hundred and fourteen generations. I figured this to be over fifteen thousand years. They eat fish, small game and jungle fruits. They do not need or use clothes. They don't even know what they are. They are a happy people with little to worry about. The river people protected the Zabadaba from intruders. They have an oral history. Their music and dances are important to them. Since they have so little, they share everything within the tribe. There is no crime because they are so harmonious. I promised that I would never disclose their location. I have visited the Zabadaba at least ten times. Every time I leave I hope they can stay invisible from modern society for one more year. The last time I visited, Zobo asked me to grant him a wish to see the future. Ladies and gentlemen, I would like to introduce Zobo, the shaman of the Zabadaba!"

The stage lights and the house lights went up. Sitting cross legged at the edge of the one step stage was Zobo in the flesh. A gasp rose from the group. He apparently had been there for the entire presentation. He stared straight ahead, unblinking.

"Yes, that's really him, Lori. Jesus!"

The people didn't know if they should applaud or not. It might scare the little guy. Miguel looked behind the stage, maybe looking for naked teenagers.

"If you have any questions, feel free to take turns asking them. Since I'm the only person in the world that can speak their language, I will translate for you."

"Mr. Zobo, have you ever been to America? If so, did you like California?"

"Zobo, Pappa domie click click —nod nod Blink —"

"Hee Hee puck puck sproik," He looked up to heaven. With arm motioning, he continued. "Clako Clako buzz wang, Zabadaba daba daba."

"This is the furthest anyone in his entire village has ventured. He has traveled many days by boat and by bus to be here tonight. His people will be praying for him every night until he gets back home."

"What can we do to help them? Can we give him clothes?"

"Shut up, Lori! They don't need your god damned clothes! They look fine the way they are! Jesus!" The voice came from behind.

Several men snickered.

Stifling a giggle, Professor Gregory continued. "They are not in need of clothes. They live an idyllic life. They have need of nothing."

"They need to find Jesus!" from a plain looking girl near the front.

"If we learned anything from history, it was The Church that killed the tribes of all of the Americas. Good intentions destroyed the Indian. They are innocents and deserve better."

All but one person in the house rolled their eyes. I think even Zobo rolled his eyes.

"Well, what can we do?" another person repeated.

"Zobo, Obie obie la wah."

"Zabadaba Hulie hulie click —blink blink —."

"Zobo asks that you enjoy their music and enjoy their leatherwork. I have assured the Zabadaba that I will revisit every year. They said they would make pouches to trade to the canoe men to assure my return. If you could, you would make Zobo proud to enjoy their music and gifts. I am sorry to say that they can only accept cash."

"I can't write you a check?"

"If the government finds anything written about these people, they will hunt them down and try to civilize them to death."

"Just give some cash, Lori. Jesus! You are beginning to sound as nutty as that Jesus freak up there! You can't trust the government. Jesus!"

Murmuring filled the room. From differing locations you could hear "damned government" and "damned church."

"To help out if you are short on dollars or pesos, the restaurant manager can charge your credit card under their 'entertainment key' to give you cash."

Bait struck and swallowed. Whale on! The crowd lined up to 'help' all they could.

I asked Miguel for another round and sat back to enjoy the sight. Thirty-eight to forty people rushing up to be the first to give all they could to help the people on the far side of that unnamed lake near that unnamed river. Protecting these helpless naked people from a ruthless nameless government was just the fight this group of sports minded, government hating, tequila guzzling sandal wearing tourist was looking for. They rallied liked the crusaders they knew they could be.

The room became a blur of activity. Donors trying to find their way to the front of the line, the plain lady behind the table selling pictures, CDs and pouches and the good professor translating his brains out. What a mural this made. Everyone was happy, especially Zobo.

Miguel arrived with the drinks. I put my arm around Matt and said, "That will be us in twenty five years."

A cool breeze found its way inside. I raised my glass to the moon. "Here's to you, Professor Hill, wherever you are!"

We have two more years to wait.

FRIENDS AND FAMILY

Chapter One: THE PUSSIFICATION OF AMERICA OBSERVED

I think I first heard the term "Pussification" years ago on Imus. At the time I snickered like I was supposed to. This was cutting edge funny and I really love clever word play.

It wasn't until one day while I was thinking of times gone by that the word came back to the front of my mind. It was like slowly waking from a warm happy dream by having someone call your name in a foreign language. You can understand there is a definite urgency in their voice, but the words make your brain work before it really wants to. "Wake up, Senor Jack! Your hair is on fire! You are dreaming too close to the sun!"

"What?" Oh, he was right. I was dreaming too close to the sun. My daydreaming was on a collision course with reality, I was beginning to see the past and the present and how they split. It took years for it to happen. Now I could see it as a time elapsed movie, like that shaky flower clip some guy shot in the fifties and we laughed at it in fourth grade.

Follow me to my and your youth:

74

Saturday morning: early to mid-sixties depending on when you were eleven.

I would wake up to the smell of burning coffee, burning bacon, burning eggs and the sound of toast having the burnt outer layer scraped off into the sink. We didn't have a smoke detector back then, just my dad yelling, "Wake up! Breakfast is ready!" It was Saturday and we had a lot to do today. We ate in silence. I have no idea what my dad was thinking during our repast, but my mind was in overdrive. I was spending the day with my dad!

This would be fun. It more than likely could be embarrassing; he had the ability to say just the right thing to embarrass a guy who was eleven, almost twelve. Last week, at the grocery store, I ran into a boy about my own age. We just stood and stared at each other and mouthed a silent hi.

My dad came up from behind me and said, "Hey, Jack! Do you know that fat kid?"

I winced in attempt to become invisible. It didn't work. Slowly, I backed away, spotted the exit and ran outside. Geez! So, as you see, it would surely be unforgettable.

My dad worked in construction. More specifically he worked with plasterers and bricklayers. His job was much like that of a roadie. He would appear on the job site a day or two before these guys. He would prepare the area for their work. He would sweep out and mask off the area, erect scaffolds, stock the work area with working platforms, buckets of water, brick and block. He unloaded sacks of cement, plaster, sand and lime from the delivery trucks. On the day of construction dad would arrive early to mix plaster or mortar, whichever was needed that day so the boys could get right to work. He would clean up after them daily and for a day or two after they left. He was always on the go, and hence his work car looked like it.

His car used to be the family car. It was a '54 Chevy station wagon. It was light blue and white on the outside and dusty white and dirty on the inside. The white dust, dried cement, and dirt came off the outer clothing my dad would wear that protected his regular clothes. When I opened the passenger side door, it would make some sort of dusty squeaky noise, followed by a loud dirty thud. Cascading from the front seat down to the floor board were many of the tools of his trade: trowels, a hammer, wide paint brushes, sandpaper, tape, wooden wedges and string. On the floor in front of my space was a five gallon bucket, dusty and dirty on both the inside and the outside. Unless I wanted to straddle this bucket all day, I would have to move it to the back. I would open the side door and push over rubber boots, rain gear and a dusty, dirty wide brimmed hard hat. I would spank my hands together and get ready to sit on my dusty cloud in the front seat. My dad stops me in mid-plop and spreads out one of his work sweatshirts for me to sit on. I reached up and removed three and a half pairs of gloves from the dash board. That left the six dollars in pennies and nickels, a wind-up clock, a plastic Jesus and his rosary.

Saturday with my dad: fun, exciting and unpredictable.

First stop, the barbershop: Superman comic books, Boys Life Magazine, Outdoor Life, Sports Illustrated and the daily newspaper, all for the reading. You could watch the *Gillette Game of the Week* on the 17 inch black and white Philco, on the top shelf of the display case, to the left of the second barber chair that was never used, that I could remember. My dad would catch up on who is doing what now and although it was boring, I would listen with one ear, just in case.

The spooky part about being downtown with my dad was the chance of being spied picking up tools, boots or sweatshirts, as they slid off the front seat and transferring them to the back seat before they could hit the ground or having him remove the white dust cloud from the seat of my dark blue pants using that eighth glove. My dad, his work car, Saturday morning and a new haircut; all fun, all dusty, all day; it was a slow and gentle rite of passage.

Next stop: the lumber yard. The same dad, the same car, same fun but strangely a different kind of possible embarrassment could be mine. We arrived at the lumber yard. We exited the car. Now, I wish we had more work junk to pick up because even though this was an embarrassing work rig thirty minutes ago, now it feels almost inadequate as a work rig. No matter how dusty it was, I knew only three years ago, the work rig was a family car with a mother and giggling sister transported in its non-dusty interior. What if people figured out our soft secret side?

First item: Two by fours. "We need two by fours, eight feet long and not that knotty shit I saw in here last week. I remember when we wouldn't even burn that shit to keep warm!" That was classic dad-speak. Classic motions would be eyeing down the edge of a piece of lumber like Robin Hood selecting his truest arrow or Minnesota Fats picking his favorite cue before his break.

Then he would tell the man we needed five sacks of cement. All the way to the next shed I would hear my dad mumble how he could have got some from work but he never would. That would be stealing.

When we arrived at the stack of sacks, it was Showtime! My dad would grab the first ninety-eight pound bag and drop it on its side. If the contents shifted effortlessly, the contents were fresh. If the contents stayed in place, the bag had encountered moisture at some point in its history. The moisture would have ruined the contents. Heaven help the lad that served up a bag of lumps to my dad.

"I wouldn't use that shit for back-fill."

We would use the back of the station wagon to carry the cement and tie the lumber to the rack on the top of the car with a dusty rope. I jumped inside, wishing the dust wasn't all lost at the barber shop. The tail of our work rig dragged on the ground as we passed all the pick-up trucks lined up outside the lumber yard.

This was a great Saturday! I was spending time with my dad and learning the ropes from a craftsman.

Now close one eye and think of that growing flower movie from back in fourth grade. A small sprout pushing its way upward through the soil, turning into a shaky plant then unfolding into a shaky orange flower, turning the past into the present.

Last week I went to get a haircut. I forgot to make an appointment. My stylist saw me sitting in the waiting room behind the giant palm plant. She motioned for me to come back. The receptionist smiled as I walked back to the chair area.

Two rows of three chairs each, the chairs were staggered for privacy. You couldn't see anyone else but you could hear as much as you wanted and more. Fashion posters were mounted on the walls. Pictures of people who you would never see in your lifetime set in their favorite poses; looking back, running in stop action, smiling to someone far away and checking the time on their watch. Hip-hop music was pushed through the Bose speakers almost loud enough to block out the lady next to me telling her stylist who was doing whom. I tried not to listen.

On my way home I had to pick up a sheet of plywood for a project in my garage. I pulled into Lowes. I had to park in the middle of the lot. A girl in a red vest greeted me as did Kenny G., lilting in the open trusses above the mercury vapor lights and exposed ductwork painted ivory white.

I picked out the plywood and placed it in the cart that had up-right rails to hold your purchase. When I got up front, I remembered I needed an extension cord, so I asked the girl at the check stand where it might be. She smiled, pointed out to the aisles and mumbled a number. Instinctively, I went in the opposite direction, transposed the numbers and found my electrical cord.

Walking passed the refrigerators, I heard a lady ask her friend if the curtains or blinds looked better with this pillow set.

That was the moment I understood that the funny sounding word was real. We have achieved the Pussification of America.

I got into my clean pick-up and drove home. On the way home, I mourned the passing of an era. The chance for a boy to hide out with his dad on a Saturday morning was gone.

What is to become of the millions of eleven year old boys without the rites of passage I enjoyed? How can they learn about their dad? No more "Guy" refuges, just refugees.

Shit!

P.S. This is absolutely true: Last week I saw a commercial on TV. It was a commercial for Lowes. It showed people dancing. Dancing at the lumberyard?

Double Shit!!

Chapter Two: FOURTH GRADE TRADE

"Where did you get the monkey's head, John?" I could have used any noun and by the end of the nine months that we called fourth grade, I know I used more nouns than I thought were available to the average ten year old. That's where I underestimated the situation. He was not average and he was not ten.

Smaller in stature and chronologically a year older than the other fourth graders, he had the advantage over the entire class. He had the advantage before he moved to the small coastal town. John spent two years in kindergarten and three years in Catholic grade school. After five years dealing with the nun, you become naturally unassuming if you must be devious.

Although we used to live only forty miles away, we were maybe five to ten years ahead in culture and technology. John found his new grade school to be a very fertile place to set up shop.

The first step upon arriving in the new school was to make friends with the biggest kid in his class. They had nothing in common except they represented the extremes in height for the class. Now that he had protection, he could rule the school, at least fourth grade.

Charm, good looks and an engaging way about him were necessary items in his skill set. You would have thought his play book was written by Tom

Sawyer. He had the ability to make a trade. If it had got out of control, I figured the rules of economics of would have taken over. There was a long list of products and services that he would have traded up for, by the end of the school day. To get to the beginning was easy but the middle part would always be blurry.

He would start the day with something small and essentially of no value in our eyes: a stick of gum, a broken toy or something he found on the beach last week. It was always his stuff, nothing stolen. I don't know if he started on the school bus or as soon as he got to the playground, but he was trading up all day.

The reason the middle part was fuzzy was because I only had his side of the story to go by. Although he would not lie, thank you, Sister Mary Elizabeth, you did have to ask the appropriate question to get the answer you were looking for.

There seems to have been some kind of trading club. I don't know if it was always there or if it was brought out in someone's backpack from Capitol City

The way I understood the rules:

Monday started a new week and a new trading session. Trades were made with items of about the same value. Both participants had to be happy with the trade, but there were no rules against salesmanship.

"That mitten sure looks good on you, Bobby!" was a good example.

After school on Friday the last trade was concluded.

Pride overtook prudence and the weekly prize was carried about the house like a "loving cup." It couldn't be helped. This represented a whole week's work. For weeks this went on.

I would ask where this new item came from only to hear that it was traded for.

"What did you trade for this?"

This would start a long litany of items that sounded even more foreign.

"I got the skateboard from a guy that I traded a basketball from another guy for a catcher's mitt."

"You live on a dirt road; you can't use a skateboard. What did it cost you?"

"I traded a mini super ball for it. It took all week."

"I think I better talk to your teacher about this."

"He doesn't care if we trade just so we don't do it in class. We just trade on the playground."

"Yeah, but what do the other parents think?" They can't be happy when their kid's toys are disappearing. I know I wouldn't."

"We just trade for things that are about the same value."

"I don't know, this still sounds like a pyramid scheme."

"Can I skateboard on the deck?"

This went on for about a month and a half. One day we got a note from the teacher stating that there would be no more trading on school property or the school bus.

"I told you, trading was bad, you're lucky some kid didn't knock you out over one of your trades."

"I've got St. James on my side; he won't let anything happen to me."

"You know, John, I don't know what they told you in Catholic school, but I don't think the saints are as active today as they might have been back in the old days. I think you probably need a better back-up plan."

"No, Dad, Simon St. James is my friend. He's the biggest kid in my class. He won't let anything happen to me. Besides I'm not trading anymore." He was shaking a small can that sounded like it contained some coins.

"Hee hee!"

"What's that?"

"What?"

"It looks like a peanut can and it sounds like it has money in it. Where did you get money?"

82

"Oh, that's just money I made selling raffle tickets."

"Who's having a raffle?"

"I am. I found these tickets in my closet and selling them for a dime a piece or three for a quarter."

"What's the prize?"

"Prize? There's no prize, I'm selling tickets."

"Do you have Simon's phone number? You might need it soon."

Chapter Three: FUN WITH MIKE AND JOHN

"Here is your order, sir, one burger special. That will be $4.95, please."

"I ordered the six dollar burger."

"That's right sir, one six dollar burger. That will be $4.95, please."

"No, I ordered the six dollar burger."

"Yes sir, you're right. It's just called a six dollar burger, but it's only $4.95."

"You don't get it. I didn't order a $4.95 burger. I want to talk to the manager!"

Then in the car:

"Is everything okay, Mike? What took so long? You look flustered."

"I don't want to talk about it."

Mike was my best friend. We worked together, we lived together, but most of all, we had fun together. We saved each other's bacon many times. We were in between jobs when we decided to go to Las Vegas to hang out with my son, John.

It went something like this:

"Hey, I just talked to John. He said we should go down for a while, said air fares are really low. Are you interested?"

"Did I ever tell you I was good at Blackjack?"

The truth was he always told me that each time we went to the casino. When we worked out of town, we went to some casino every other night. The other truth was: no, he wasn't very good at Blackjack. Not that I was any better. I just tried not to say anything about it.

I got on the internet and found cheap airfare; I also found some discounted rooms on The Strip.

In a couple days we were on our way. John picked us up at the airport and took us to our new digs. We stowed our luggage in our room and went downstairs to the tables.

I always had fun playing Blackjack with Mike and John. Mike with his "Six Dollar Hamburger" seriousness and John with his "take no prisoners" sense of humor made playing Blackjack a laugh riot. It was a "milk shooting out your nose" laugh riot.

We would choose an empty Blackjack table. Mike would sit in the chair on the dealer's left. This chair is called first base. First base is the first to get cards as the dealer works from their left to their right.

John would sit in the fourth chair from the left. This middle chair is called center field. For some reason, there are a lot of references to baseball in Blackjack. This middle chair is in the center of the field of players.

I would sit on the dealer's far right side. This chair is called third base. Sitting on third base has the responsibility of playing against the dealer in order to save the whole table. The third baseman must watch the dealer's hand, and if it looks as though the dealer must take another card, the third baseman will not take a card for himself in hopes the dealer draws a high card forcing him to go over twenty-one. I always play third base to insure someone who knows what's going on is covering this responsibility.

The odds on Blackjack are the best in the casino, but you can only win what you risk. It is possible to play for hours at a time, winning and losing the same chips over and over. Knowing this, we would settle in on a table and play and laugh for hours.

Mike, with his bushy mustache and deadpan expression, would always look at his cards, twitch his mustache as if he was reciting the rules of Blackjack and play accordingly. Mike's tempo would pace our game, stretching out the play and saving us money in the long run. It was impossible for any dealer to speed up Mike.

If the dealer looked like he or she might be trying to push Mike, John would direct his chatter at the dealer. John would begin asking the dealer about receiving free cards. The casinos no longer give away cards; they sell them in the gift shop. The free card rant was always entertaining. John could remember getting cards last month and was certain it was here. He would ask me if I would want cards. I always thought that would be a great idea, something to take home as a souvenir.

When other players joined our table, it was Showtime. Mike would talk to the women, offering them a stay at his imaginary horse ranch back home. When Mike and I worked out of town, at least once a week there would be a young woman standing at our front door with her luggage ready to go to the horse ranch. He never learned.

John could schmooze with anyone who sat next to him, local or traveler, winner or loser, joking or commiserating as needed. It was always fun to watch John.

My job was easy and fun. Watch these guys and make sure that I don't take the dealer's high card.

On this trip, there seemed to be a certain buzz in Vegas, a red colored buzz. After the second day of watching this red blur in town, I asked one of the women at our table what was going on.

"What brings you girl girls to Vegas? The Blackjack?"

"Ah geez no, I'm here wit' the ole man. He's ooaver there smokin' seegars and playin pooaker wit' da boys. We're here for the game on Saturday, you know, the Wiscaahnsin game."

Oh, that's right. John said he had a shot at getting us tickets for the game. The game was the Wisconsin vs. UNLV football season opener. That's why every other person in town was wearing red; it was Wiscaahnsin red.

Betting was very heavy that week. As the planes from the Midwest emptied at the airport and filled the hotels. The lines to the front desk of the casino hotels always border the Book Board area. The Book Board is where you would place a bet on a particular sporting game.

With everyone from out of town betting on the Red team, it was incumbent on the citizenry of Las Vegas to cover the bets by betting on their Rebels. It was a gambling showdown that turned into one of those perfect storms you read about.

This perfect storm could be mapped out this way: A high pressure area blows in from the east. This high pressure zone is being pushed by a Big Ten, top twenty rated football team with swelling pride all the way from the Great Lakes region.

The storm clouds are meeting another ridge of high pressure. This time it is the hot dessert winds that are accustomed to not moving, just swirling in a circle around the oasis, butting heads as needed.

Then there is the underlying high pressure that holds the big buildings on the strip together. This pressure is controlled by the buildings themselves, changing the fluctuating odds that are securing equity.

One man's stubbornness is another man's steadfastness. From my experience, steadfastness is a Midwestern trait. Now when I say Midwestern, I'm really meaning a Germanic based, narrow minded, pride driven, don't tell me what to do, happy-go-lucky attitude. If this steadfastness has money to put down on a sure thing, get out of the way.

To recap, this is what happened: Red money from the Midwest clashing with local pride betting from LV, trying to stay ahead of odd setting from the big hotels, equal this Perfect Storm.

John got us tickets to the game. The ride there was a chartered bus provided by the manager of John's favorite bar. The bus had an open bar on the way to the game.

Everything is forty-five minutes away from everywhere in Las Vegas. Saturday afternoon went like this; the game started at seven, we got to the bus at two. Some riders started drinking at seven in the morning, some on Wednesday.

Forty-five minutes and three beers later, we were at the stadium. We exited the bus and walked across the parking lot. The first three steps were not that bad. Then we realized it was one hundred and four degrees Fahrenheit. The three beers were now dust on our foreheads and nape of our necks.

Forty-five minutes later we were in our seats, thirty yard line, two thirds up. One hundred four degrees outside in the open air equates to about one hundred twenty-four in a bowl shaped stadium in the sun, full of people, without a breeze. It was hot!

The people in our section looked familiar; they were the same happy people from the bus. The free alcohol on the bus got our section quite animated and full of team spirit although it was hard to decide which team we represented.

The big guys, three rows down, were really having a good time. It seemed the big guys in front of us had started drinking Wednesday. I'm sure they forgot they were at a public location, not that it would make a difference. I'm sure.

I thought I might need a whistle and a striped shirt or a chair and a whip. My problem was I had to keep track of Mike and John. Mike was getting a bit exercised over the way the big guys three rows down were treating their dates. John was easier to take control of because he knew of the big guys, three rows down. He knew them from the bar. He told me they worked security for special events on The Strip. He didn't have to point out that they were big because they were three rows down, and we were still looking up to see them.

The football game was competing for the attention of the people in our section. Girls were being tossed about like so many Frisbees between big guys.

They squealed and shrieked while they were airborne. Mike snapped, growled and snarled as this took place.

"They are disrespecting those women!"

Avoiding the obvious irony, "Yes, but the girls seem to be enjoying it, Mike?" Then: Wow! Did you see that play?"

Unfortunately one of the big guys stood up and mooned the crowd.

Check, please!

It was my job to defuse this bomb. "Hey, Mike, let's go out for a smoke."

We went to the designated smoking area; an open air porch-like area filled with over a hundred smokers huddled around their lit cigarettes hoping to cool off. We could hear the crowd roaring, but since the crowd was split about fifty-fifty, we couldn't tell who just scored.

"Mike, if it's okay with you and John, we could leave at halftime, go back to the bar and watch the rest of the game on TV. We could beat the crowd!"

We got back to our seats. "John, let's sneak out early and go back to the bar."

"Sure, Pops. No problem."

Forty five minutes to walk out to the main street. We discovered there wasn't a taxi driver in town that thought it would be a great idea to hang around the area in case three guys wanted to leave the most popular game this year at half time. Go figure.

We finally got a cab. John stayed on top of the cab driver to make sure he took the cheapest way back.

When we got back to the bar, we were cooled down and ready for a beer. We got stools at the bar since most of the patrons were at the game. The game was on ESPN2. There was still time left in the fourth quarter. We watched the Wisconsin lead build to twenty-seven to seven with just minutes to go.

I went to the restroom and came back in two minutes. When I returned to my stool, there was a different game on. "Mike, did they change the channel?"

"No, Jack, the game is still on."

A game was on but not ours. Pretty soon some of the group started to return to the bar.

They said the game was called because there was a power outage.

Power outage?

Anywhere on the planet and the story is over. We are in Las Vegas, not the end of the story. Here's where you have to tilt your head a little and squint your eyes to see the dolphin in the picture of palm trees. You remember those pictures at the malls in the nineties.

Back up, back up! Remember the perfect storm! Remember where you are. Remember the Book Board. Now read the back of your betting ticket, the one you got when you put money on your favorite team. In the fine print down toward the bottom there is a disclaimer. It states that the ticket is void in case of a game that is not a complete regulation game.

The college people declared the winner to be Wisconsin by virtue of having a score of twenty-seven to seven over UNLV when the lights went out with only minutes to go.

Back up some more. You will soon realize your gambling ticket is worthless. Everyone's ticket is worthless. According to the gaming commission, the game is not over, there were still minutes on the clock, and there is no winner.

All the people who bet on their favorite red team with their red money lost their red bet, as did the local people who put up their local money.

Some of the things to ponder: How did the lights go out? Why wasn't there a technician on site who could turn the lights back on? If the game would have ended the way it was supposed to, how much money would have been paid out? Who ended up with the money? How much did the technician make by taking his break when he did? How many new wranglerettes will be waiting at the imaginary horse ranch at Mike's apartment? When can we do this again? I had a blast!

Just remember their slogan: "Whatever you bet in Vegas stays in Vegas."

Chapter Four: NEWSPAPER CLIPPINGS

I grew up feeling sorry for the people of Iowa. I decided early on that for one reason or another, they were growing the stupidest offspring on the planet. Let me explain. My mom's family lived in the Midwest. She had a favorite who lived in Iowa. Her aunt had no children of her own and doted on my mom and us.

As children, we received plenty of attention at Christmas. Every year she would send money for my mom to buy presents for us. She also sent handmade items for us to wear, usually knitted. I was just thankful my knitted item didn't match my sisters' items, like theirs always did.

My mom's aunt was also her lifeline to her past and her family. They corresponded almost weekly by letter. My mom would receive an air mail envelope. These were specially printed envelopes with a picture of an airplane that would inform the people in the post office in which bin to place this puffy nearly overweight link to "Back Home."

The envelopes were puffy because, besides being ten pages of handwritten —both sides —family information; there were always four or five newspaper clippings enclosed.

The clippings fell into two categories; recipes, which were stored in the cookbook and "other" which were stored in the Bible. Both books were twice their original thickness due to these clippings.

The recipes also fell into two categories; Hot Dish and Jell-o mold. My mom would try out these One Dish Wonders on Saturday evenings. They were hit and miss, mostly miss. My mom always told her aunt the recipes were great, hence more recipes next week.

The "other" clippings were filed away in the Old Testament. I always thought they were placed there to slow down any burglars who were trying to find my mom's "secret hiding place" —page twenty-five of the New Testament. She always had money stored on page twenty-five; not much, just enough to buy the extra ingredients for next week's Saturday special. I had visions of those fat burglars, you know, the ones who followed Scrooge McDuck around, wearing those burglar/Lone Ranger masks, reading the hundreds of news clippings while the police politely waited for them to finish.

It wasn't until I got older that I understood how the clippings were to be used.

Remember WWII? Few people know how we really beat the Germans. OSS agents snuck into Berlin and broke into Der Spiegel, a well-known publication at the time. They printed a front-page story stating the Germans had lost the war. Adolph Hitler read the early edition, shouted Ach Nein, ran to the suicide wing of his underground bunker and shot himself.

Why was this trickery so effective? Because, everyone knows, Germans believe everything they read in print. Trust me. I know this to be true.

Soon after you become aware of the world outside of your family, you want to participate in it or at least observe it. This is when I learned exactly what those "other" clippings were and why they were being protected by God in our Bible.

These newspaper clippings were "Exhibit A." They were sent all the way from Iowa, by airmail, to my mom, from her aunt. They were possibly only a curiosity to start with, but by the time they spent several years becoming sanctified in my mom's Bible and the fact they were printed, the articles clipped from the Iowa Gazette were the trump cards any mother needed to thwart logic.

Let's say for example, you wanted to do something "risky" like ride your bike here or there and you were only twelve and lived on a gravel road in the country.

Nope, can't do it, too dangerous.

What?

It seems there was a twelve year old kid in Des Moines who died riding his bike to town at noon, wearing a white jacket, a football helmet, while astride his bright red Schwinn with playing cards clothes pinned to his wheels.

What? Impossible!

After thirty seconds of feverish rummaging through Deuteronomy, aha! "Exhibit A" for your discouragement!

Oh man!

Unfolding the Iowa Gazette piece from who knows when, with her perfect "See I told you so!" look on her face, my mom would let me read the headline: "Iowa Boy Rides His Bike on Road to Death". It you read the whole story, you would probably discover that the poor lad was struck by lightning, tornado or a meteorite but it didn't matter. "BOY, BIKE, DEATH." That was all that mattered. It was in print, it was true, you were thwarted, end of argument.

BB gun, fishing pole, roller skates, it could be any verb or noun, there would be a newspaper clipping that would rain on your parade. There was no use trying to get around the bad luck or pure stupidity of those kids from Iowa.

You would think that there would be a whole generation of Iowans lost to freak accidents. Who will grow our corn? How will we manage? How can they be so dumb?

These objection pieces only worked one way, against me. I'm not paranoid, I can prove it.

We had a fireplace in our house, and my dad and I would cut wood all summer and autumn and haul it home in eight foot pieces. Sometimes these oak logs would be two feet in diameter. Oak is a very dense, very heavy wood. It was always more than a one guy job to wrestle these logs on then off the trailer, even for my dad. So I would help my dad, which I enjoyed. We were two guys doing guy work on Saturdays throughout the summer, autumn and early winter. Since we gathered the wood at a time when we could drive the tractor to the tree grove, we would just stockpile these logs near the house for future processing. When the rains made it too muddy to drive the tractor to the trees, we would pull up the old Allis Chalmers near the house and attach the buzz saw.

The buzz saw was a thirty-six inch saw blade attached to an axle which was attached to an iron framework. On the back of this framework was a movable bed. It moved out and in. Out to load the log on the bed then slowly in to cut off a slab of the log. The blade's axle had a small but wide wheel on the opposite end as the blade. This wheel would be connected to a matching wheel on the tractor by means of a wide drive belt. The drive belt was multi-plied rubber and canvas belt stitched together with a leather lacing. It was about six feet long when it was laced together and there was a heavy metal wheel that rode on the top of this loop that would take out the slack of the belt when the blade spun. The tractor's PTO system made the belt move which spun the blade. The throttle would be set so the blade would attain working speed; it produced a very high pitched whir.

My dad and I would heft up one of the oak logs and place it on the table and my dad would push the log into the blade. My job was to hold the piece of the log that was being cut off. When the sixteen inch long piece was cut off I would catch the piece, not letting it hit the ground and toss it onto the pile to my left and come back to grab the next piece. My movements were restricted; I couldn't allow the piece of wood to pull me down and expose my soft fontanel to the high speed blade. I also couldn't return too quickly to my position, because I might swing my arms into the blade, yet I had to hold the piece of wood near the center which would put my hands between six and eight inches from the edge of the high speed blade. It was spooky, real spooky.

We would spend Saturday getting everything set up; tractor, table and belt. Then my dad would sharpen the blade with a file.

Now close your eyes. It would take all day Saturday to get everything set up. Are your eyes still closed? Good, now you are ready.

My dad would get home at about five. In the winter, five o'clock is dark, very dark. We had a hundred watt light bulb screwed into the side of the house. It didn't help very much. We would cut wood for an hour before dinner. Always dark, sometimes raining, sometime windy would be catching and tossing wood in robot fashion, before we knew about robots. I am certain it was dangerous. I know I blanked much of it from my memory.

I do remember going through my mom's Bible one day looking for a newspaper clipping about some kid from Iowa getting cut in half with a buzz saw. No such luck! Maybe all the kids were killed before wood cutting season.

So as you can see, I grew up with a complete distain for the Hawkeyes and their stupid kids. And don't get me started on the phobias and beliefs of the German people.

Chapter Five: MRS. SCHMEDLEY

"I'm so mad at those pitchers," speaking of her favorite major league baseball team. "Our batters get a small lead and the coach pulls out the opening pitcher and puts in one of those new guys. They are like amateurs. Those guys load up the bases, and one of their guys hit them all in and we lose the game."

"I know, Mom, it's frustrating."

"I get so mad!" Holding her eighty-eight year old hands in front of her, "I could just choke that pitcher." Her hands are shaking. "Well, you know, I really couldn't"

"Well no, of course you couldn't…that would be…mur…"

"I couldn't…because I have this arthritis and I can't make my fingers work so well."

One time at the market, she was pushing her cart when she almost ran into another woman, pushing her cart from around a display.

"They should put horns on these carts."

The woman smiled and nodded in agreement. She was probably wondering how one would affix a safety device on the carts. What she didn't know was that my mom meant steer horns to clear the way for her passage.

I had heard all the stories.

One time the manager of the dairy made a sixty-five mile trip to bring her a box full of dairy products because she called and reported that she didn't quite like the taste of their milk.

"You guarantee your products, don't you?"

"Yes ma'am, we certainly do!"

"Well, I'm not satisfied. What are you going to do about it?"

He brought her gallons of milk, pounds of butter, half and half and yogurt. She made him take back the yogurt because she doesn't like yogurt.

Then there was the time she called the bank inquiring about a service charge being levied on one of her accounts. The girl explained how she was sent a letter two months ago, stating that any account under twenty-five thousand dollars would be charged a monthly fee.

Instead of addressing the problem head on by ending the account in question which would certainly mitigate the bank's money grabbing, she chose to confuse the girl with the following:

"How am I supposed to get twenty-five thousand dollars?"

More than likely facing more blinking lights on her phone, the girl gave up and awarded her two months fee reimbursement.

I always feel like an accomplice when I take her to the bank or the store, but my job is simply to drive, usher and amplify as needed. I still feel uneasy watching her work. The public is completely unaware and hopelessly outgunned.

She usually insists on going to the bank in person. It's not that she completely mistrusts the postal system, she believes in the personal touch when dealing with the bank. It's not just the bank, it's dealing with others. She works best in person, even better than on the phone. Watching is truly worth the ticket.

I parked in front on the bank. She opened her fourteen and a half pound purse and pulled out her blue and white handicapped parking permit. I hooked it on the rearview mirror as she told the story of her permit. When she finished, I got out and walked to the other side of the pick-up, opened her door, helped her out and handed her the cane. We walked inside.

I felt as invisible as Chewbacca standing next to Yoda, which is what we must have looked like.

As we walked into the bank, she pointed to a teller behind the counter.

"She's my friend, Brenda." Her friend smiled and waved, but her friend was busy and we waited in the line of another teller.

She only needed to withdraw money from one of her accounts, something that could have been done in the drive-thru, but there's no fun in that.

"Good morning, Mrs. Schmedley," smiled the girl as she looked at the paperwork. "Do you want to make a withdrawal?"

"Yes, I do." She looked, sweet talking to the teller. Her head was tilted up so they could see each other over the counter, through the small double doors. The doors were next to the name plate that stated the teller's name was Molly.

"Say, I noticed you have some stuffed animals here. What are they for?" She pointed to a plush toy horse.

This was the trigger that the teller was waiting for so that she could use the canned pitch for opening a new account.

"They are a free gift for opening a new account here at the bank."

I really hate the term "free gift," but the teller looked so proud that she got the speech out and correct. I couldn't interrupt, plus I'm just the observer and the show is about to begin.

"I have three accounts here plus several CDs. Am I eligible?"

The girl smiled weakly trying not to repeat the word "new" more than six times.

"I will...ask um...Brenda!" she ran toward the back of the room. There was a buzz involving three other people. It lasted several minutes. She then returned. "Why certainly, Mrs. Schmedley, here you go and here's your receipt, thank you."

My mom is motionless. She is holding the stuffed horse under her arm. She clears her throat, looks up to Molly and says, "I need two of them."

"I'm sorry Mrs. Schmedley, there is a limit."

"But, I need two of them. I have two great grandchildren."

"They could share it," Molly suggested.

"Oh no, that wouldn't work. One of them lives here and one lives in Nevada."

"Well, but..."

"So you see, I need two of them." Then the Jedi magic began. "What would you have me do? They can't share it because they live so far from each other, can they?"

These questions are completely off target for a reason. The brain of the victim has been given a completely illogical question to ponder while trying to also defend the Empire hide-out.

The usual response is, "What?" This was no exception.

The cane is held like a staff swaying back and forth, also meant to mesmerize.

The eyebrows of the teller arched beyond the safety point, this could be permanent. Beads of sweat began to breakout on her young forehead. "Brr Enn Daa" formed on her lips without a sound being uttered. It was all over now. I tried not to look involved. At this point I wished I had Jedi powers of invisibility.

The girl reached under the counter and brought out another stuffed horse. Head down, she pushed the toy trough the little doorway. I thanked Molly and carried the horse out to the pick-up.

Mrs. Schmedley walked victoriously to the parking lot, cane in one hand and horse/football under her other arm. She resembled the guy on the Heisman trophy. I opened the passenger door and she climbed in.

All the way back to her house, I felt like Clyde Barrow. I kept looking behind us.

99

Chapter Six: BINGO BOXING

In the back ground I could hear:

"Ed Benedict, the Canadian ham actor, received rave reviews for his portrayal of the father of Holly Days, the saucy young breakfast waitress in the Off-Broadway production of *Do You Want Lids on These*?"

As I was hammering out another up-to-the-minute hard-hitting story, the kind my readers were used to, I was listening to the morning news on my TV. I tried to ignore it as I composed.

My story started in the hospital. Looking for my friend, I slowly walked through the ER. I was exposed to the most intimate parts of people's lives coming through the thin curtains of the cubicles.

I tried not to listen, it didn't work:

"Do you remember anything else, Mrs. Bradford?

"I remember having amnesia."

Another:

"I told my doctor the medicine he prescribed was worthless. I told him I thought he was a quack trying to cure me with that garbage. He recommended a suppository,"

From another cubicle:

"What do you mean the tattoo won't come off? I got a new girlfriend now and her name isn't Sparkle."

Snapping out of my daydreaming, a small nurse confronted me.

"Can I help you, sir?"

I made a mental note. Nurses ask if they can help you, the lady at Macys asks if she may help you. I'll think about that later.

"Yes, I'm here to pick up my friend, Mr. Benedict."

"Oh, the rake victim, he's in number seven. Follow me, please."

"You know, it sounds of funny the way you say it."

"There is nothing funny about a broken nose."

"No, you're right, absolutely."

"Here he is."

"Ed, are you ready to go home now?

"I nust nave to nign nome napers."

"Okay, I'm just going outside to bring the car around."

My wife just came back from her daily walk. I stopped writing. "You look refreshed. You must have had a good walk."

"What do you mean by that?"

"Nothing, nothing. I just a…Hey! Remember, we're taking my mom to play bingo today."

"Oh, yeah."

I know my wife likes to hang out with my mom, it's just when we go to the casino, my wife has to sit in the backseat of our small car.

"If you wanted a contortionist, you should have married that circus girl."

"Oh yeah, Sparkle, the circus girl. Hmm."

"What?"

"Nothing."

The Indian casino lies along the second busiest highway in our state. It was the second busiest highway before the casino was built, which is probably why it was built there. Tricky Red Devils!

On the way to the casino, my mom suggested that the on-coming traffic must all be coming from the casino. I tried to explain that there were other attractions serviced by this highway besides the casino, like the ocean.

"What?"

"Nothing."

When we arrive at the casino, my mom opens her fourteen and a half pound purse and pulls out the blue and white handicapped parking permit. I find a parking space and hang the permit on my rear-view mirror. I exit the driver's side and go around to help my mom out of the passenger's seat. I guide her toward the sidewalk and try to help my wife out of the backseat. I push the seat forward and offer my wife a hand.

"I've got it! It's just tight back here. What are you looking at?"

"Nothing, it's just that your ear looks kind of red."

"It's from my knee; I told you it was tight back here."

When we entered the building, we instinctively turned right toward the bingo hall.

We walked down the wide walkway lined with reproductions of old photographs of our only Americans walking along a river bank with bundles secured to their backs. This was their contribution to our society; showing us how to do the work by just doing it and not worrying about a wheel or any other contrivance to do the work for them.

I briefly wait in line at the ATM, a European invention that came along right after the wheel.

We obtain our bingo boxes and select our seats. The boxes are electronic bingo computers that display the games, make it easier to play and save six thousand trees a day by not making bingo sheets.

Our seats are the same seats my folks used forever. My mom sets up camp at her table. She sports a victorious smile because no one got up early enough today to sit in her chair two and a half hours before the games start. We bide our time playing solitaire, a video-game offered on the bingo box. We eat hot dogs and drink diet cola.

The games begin. For the next two and a half hours we sit and watch our bingo boxes playing without ever being touched by us. We watch and wait for the prompt from the bingo box that tells us to get excited and get ready to yell bingo! The prompt rarely sounds and the few times it does, someone is getting bingo somewhere behind us and the noise drowns out the prompt sound. Actually, the sound doesn't come from the bingo winner but the groans from the other box watchers who just got their own prompt.

Eighteen games, eighteen times we remain silent, eighteen dashed hopes for each of us. We walk out to the car. I help fold my wife into the backseat again and we were on our way. We were silent for a few minutes. We pump up our spirits on the way home. There's always next time.

I try to remind my mom about the ocean when she sees all the traffic going to the casino.

We will do this again soon.

Chapter Seven: STATE SPONSORED JARGON REASSIGNMENT

Yesterday, he was smoking pot, today he is medicating. What a difference a day makes.

I want to start with a sincere explanation. My friend has a very terrible disease. He has lost body parts to cancer and will probably lose more. He is in pain and just the uncertainty of his situation is mind numbing. This is not the story. I want you to understand that his health issue is how we got to where we are starting the story.

I have other friends in far less dire situations that have preceded us in the journey to Portland to obtain their Golden Ticket. I am now on the freeway driving Charlie Bucket to Portland to get his Golden Ticket. He read all of the brochures and memorized all that he read. It was important. It was important because he must be able to speak a new language; The Language of Medical Marijuana."

All the way to Portland, young Charlie was practicing his new lingo. Never, since college, have I witnessed someone conjugating verbs so hard. His eyes were closed tight and his head bobbed with each syllable; "Medicine, Medicate, Medicare. No. not Medicare, oh, I'm never going to get this right."

"That's okay, we're almost there."

"But what if there's a test? What if the doctor doesn't think I'm ready? What if the doctor doesn't give me a prescription?"

"I'm pretty sure you will get your prescription. You did your paperwork. You can still fog up a mirror. You have a hundred dollars in your pocket."

I sat in my pickup while Charlie went inside to see the "doctor." He told me it might take two hours. I sat back and offered my soul to Morpheus.

Remember what I said about people in need of pain relief. I would drive all of the people to Portland if they needed it. That's not what this is about. This is also not about whether or not marijuana should or should not be legalized. What this is about is the changing of terminologies because of a change in perspective.

It only took one hour. Charlie let himself into the cab of the pickup. If I thought he was a chatterbox on the way to Portland, WOW! He found another gear. The problem was I had to catch up with the language change. The words he used were not foreign, I heard them every day. It's just that they stood for something other than what I had used them for in everyday life.

What I earlier referred to as a Golden Ticket is now called a prescription; he received it from his doctor. His buddy, Bobby, with whom he used to smoke pot, is now called his Service Provider. His pot is now called medicine and you get it at the Medication Dispensary. The act of smoking pot is now called medicating, and his pipe is now called an applicator.

We traveled eight blocks and he took his prescription out of his notebook at least eight times. Each time he read an important part of the document. The prescription was a state form filled out and signed by the doctor. It was eight and a half inches by eleven inches full of information and regulations. The blank spaces were filled out in black ink and denoted the legal name and address of the patient and the dosage as prescribed by the doctor.

Some of the rules included where to find medicating groups, where you could interact with other patients. These groups would help dispense —share — excess medicine to patients who might need more until their crop comes in.

There were also rules on how much medicine one could carry on their person at any given time —two and a half pounds —and how much their service provider can have on hand at any given time in his name —another two and a half pounds.

"You better get that thing laminated before you wear it out."

"I plan on it! Can I ask you to do one more thing before we get home?"

"Sure, go ahead."

"Can we stop at the medication dispensary so I can pick up some medicine?"

"Okay, but we're not stopping at the match store."

"What?"

We pulled into the dispensary, nee Smoke Shop. Again, I waited in the car. Three minutes later Charlie returned.

"Ah, man! They wouldn't fill my prescription!"

"Why not?"

"I need to get it stamped by the Department of Health. I told them the doctor said it was legal. They said until I get it stamped, they couldn't fill my prescription, and today is a state holiday. Ah, man! The doctor said I'm supposed to start medicating right away. I'm already two doses behind schedule. God dammit."

"You'll probably have to stay up late just to catch up."

"What?"

To further verify his claim he again took out this prescription.

"The doctor said I have to take two doses before I get up in the morning."

I was thinking that if I had two doses, I probably wouldn't want to get up in the morning. Hmmm.

"I just can't figure out what am I going to do between now and Monday. God dammit!"

"Well, here's a dumb question. What did you do yesterday?"

"What?"

This time I responded.

"You know, what did you do yesterday before it was medicine?"

"What do you mean? Geez, what am I going to do?"

"Listen, Charlie. Calm down. Listen to what I'm saying. What did you do when it wasn't medicine, you know, when it was just pot?"

"Oooh, yeah! I get it! Can I get you to do me one more favor?"

"Sure, Charlie. What is it?"

"Can you drop me off at my friend Bobby's house?"

"Isn't Bobby your care giver?"

"Not until I get this thing stamped. Now he's just my supplier."

"Well, when you go to your group session and someone needs an "I Don't Care Provider," sign me up."

"What?"

"Never mind. Where does Bobby live?"

Chapter Eight: GOLFING WITH FRIENDS

When I think of golfing, my mind travels back to the early nineties. I was never very good at golf, but I had a lot of fun and especially when I teamed up with three guys I met through a friend. Sundays worked out good for us. I had nothing to do on Sundays and they were Jewish, so it was like their Saturday.

Daniel was a short pear shaped man. He was a high school teacher and a very polite and gentle man. Jim was about six foot three. He was younger than us and very athletic. He was a very good golfer. He also taught at the high school and even though he was twice the golfer we were combined, he was quite patient with us. Michael was about ten years older than me. He was some kind of salesman, very congenial but certainly not a golfer. He tried hard, but you could still see him counting down the steps necessary to strike a golf ball each time he addressed his ball.

The course was an older Presidential course on the other side of town. It was the drawing point to a retirement village. We liked it because if we got there early enough on Sunday morning, we could play before the old timers got out of bed. This was important because they always thought we were interlopers taking advantage of their 'hidden' public hide-out. We also had to start early because of Michael.

We would start at eight o'clock, the first tee time available. Jim would call earlier in the week to make arrangements.

In the clubhouse, Michael would detail all the practicing he did during the week. He would be shadow putting in the pro shop as we drank our morning coffee. We offered Michael first tee honors every week. I think we all secretly knew this would be the only time he would legally be able to tee off first all morning. He would always argue with us, offering the honors to each of us in order until he ran out of excuses.

I remember watching Curly Howard golf and how hilarious he was. When someone you know is standing nearby trying their best and yet appearing even funnier than the Master, you can't laugh out loud, no matter what. Three of us would catch each other examining the grass around our feet, thinking of the saddest moments we could conjure, avoiding the giggles that were suppressed within. If one of us would have cracked, there would be certain unstoppable pandemonium.

Although we were not dressed for success, we wore casual sports clothing and looked like we fit into the golf scene, except Michael. He wore light yellowish green slacks, black golf shoes and an old brown cable knit sweater that looked like it once belonged to his sister. Bespectacled with large thick lenses mounted in light brown plastic rims, he wore a straw golfing hat. The flat brimmed hat looked like the one once worn by Chi Chi Rodriguez. Added to this respectable hat was a small plastic golf ball glued to the top and a small greens flag. It was encircled by a strip of green felt to resemble a putting green.

Before we started, Michael asked us how we liked his lucky hat. Passing on judgment, we encouraged him to begin. Michael would select his club from the bag. He peeled off the club cover which was once his sister's knee sock and waggled as he approached the tee box.

Bending down to place his ball and tee, the green hat band became unglued on one end. The band unrolled and hung down in front of Michael's face. It was held from completely unraveling by his lucky golf pin, a small figure of a little gold golfer swinging a club placed dead center in front on his green hat band. Undaunted, Michael would blow up at the band just like Shemp used to blow his hair out of the way when he was also trying to concentrate.

"I got this, I got this," he would say.

Wrapping the band back into place with his left hand, he addressed the ball. Then the counting began. Like an eighth grader counting the steps of a polka during Rhythms Class, Michael would count down the steps to his first swing. Ball centered, feet at shoulder's width and aimed at the pin, he battled the hat band again, now just snapping and twisting his head to force the hat band back in place. A deep cleansing breath and a hard swing of his driver, a loud swoosh sound and the club head skipped off the ground four inches behind his ball, it smacked as it hit the ball. We all shaded our eyes as we tried to follow its arc in the bright blue sky.

"Wow! Did you see that? Did you see how straight it flew?"

"Yeah, Michael, that practice paid off," one of us would say.

Twenty-eight paces straight ahead laid Michael's ball. Eight more of these machinations and we were at the first green. Somehow in between, we would get in our shots. There would always be some old timer, carrying his three clubs in on hand and a cup of coffee in the other that we would let play through. Three of us would be kicking invisible rocks while Michael chatted up the old timer as he puffed through.

"What a great day for golf!"

Nine holes in the time it should take for eighteen, we would have to convince the guy at the club house that we only went through once. Eventually, he figured out we had our own handicap.

Michael would be the first to set up next week's match. We would look at his oversized eyeballs behind his oversized glasses as they blinked, waiting for our response. We all pledged to return next week. Michael promised to practice at least four days next week.

We played every Sunday for four months. After winter arrived, we disbanded.

None of us could tell this story to anyone. Who would believe us? It was too fantastic, and we would look like idiots for letting it go on for so long. But it really was fun. It was a study in patience and humility, but it also built a comradeship that I will never forget.

Daniel passed away and Jim moved out of town. I imagine Michael is still practicing and has yet to fix his hat.

It looks like it's about time to dust off my clubs and get ready for spring golf. Each year before I go out again I think about those Sunday mornings and all the simple fun I shared with my golfing friends.

Chapter Nine: MY SMART FRIENDS

I enjoy doing crossword puzzles, but I wish I was as good as my wife. I always thought I was a good player because I used a pen instead of a pencil, but my wife pointed out that with all the cross outs and write overs on my puzzles, they resemble a Rorschach test.

"I don't think it's that bad," I countered.

"What do you think that looks like, Jack?" holding up my puzzle from yesterday.

"It looks like a butterfly killing the neighbor kids with an Uzi."

"Now you're just dreaming"

She also knows all of those trivial things that are stumpers in the across clues, they are the tougher ones you know.

"Honey! Who was Jesus' brother-in-law? Seven letters."

"Seymour."

"Seymour? Well, it fits."

I always feel comfortable in my little comfort bubble. I know I am the smartest person in my chair. I may not know everything in the world, but I do know people who do know the answers and they are right next to me or just a phone call away.

One of these people is a friend of mine named Thornton. Thornton is not his real name. His real name is some unpronounceable Armenian name, but everyone knows him as Thornton.

I enjoy talking with him and try to meet him every time he's in town. We will meet at a local pub downtown and sit outside so Thornton can smoke. He loves to smoke and drink whiskey; expensive smokes and cheap whiskey. He would always try to explain the logic behind pampering oneself with a Nat Sherman Oval and drinking the whiskey of the people, whichever was the cheapest bar whiskey.

I met Thornton twenty-five years ago. I was bar tending at a hotel restaurant in Portland. Thornton was the keynote speaker at a function in the hotel down the street. After his speech but before the reception, he came in for a double and a couple Ovals. I was caught up on my side work and looking for a conversation. I moved down the bar, emptied his ashtray and introduced myself.

He was in town to promote a book. He was a very distinguished looking man in his fifties. Black and white hair combed straight back and just long enough to stay there. Swarthy looks and muscular frame made him appear extremely believable. If he said something, he looked as though he was capable of doing it.

He didn't like to talk about his past, but he had a very envious list of experiences. I had read about him and wanted to interview him just for my own edification. I wanted to ask about his days marching in Selma and nights studying with Saul Bellow.

I guess being Armenian gives one a predisposition to fighting for the rights of others. Since before its time as part of the Roman Empire until the early 1990's, countries of the world have waited in line to march in and beat up the Armenian people. They had about two years of freedom before the Turks moved in in 1920 to give them their worst beating. If it hadn't been for their independence in 1991, Iceland might have manned up for their turn at the Armenian speed bag.

I used Thornton as an encyclopedia. I would ask a question and he would tell me everything he knew about the subject, usually from firsthand knowledge. He would have been there. From our first encounter on, we would spend hours drinking and making me a bit more informed. I am excited every time he is in town and after he leaves, I spend hours in the library reading more on the subjects.

This time it was going to be the "Occupy" situation. I always said it was incumbent on our young people to take the time to investigate and hold powers accountable for their practices. We, the working people, have to keep working while the young educated non-workers keep vigilant eye on the boiler and let us know what's going on.

I know we got cheated during the "Me Decade" but this group of young people is working overtime for us. I wanted to be with them, but my schedule didn't cooperate plus I couldn't find one of those little hats in my size, seven and seven eights, yeah big. I think it would have taken three Peruvian llamas to make one that big.

I asked what his opinion of the Occupy Movement was. Thornton said that the movement actually started in 1996 with a showdown in Bolivia with the World Bank and their influence on the weak and greedy government of a country so far away. He said when he was there, of course, the World Bank gave money to the government of Bolivia and insisted they employ certain contractors to put in water/sewer systems and these companies charged the people twenty percent of their monthly income just to drink water. Thornton spent seven months in prison, of course, in Cochabamba. He would have gotten out earlier, but he was educating his fellow prisoners in international law and civil rights.

Later, the movement followed the Monsanto controversy about the company owning all the seeds for the farmers of the world to plant for the next year's crops. Ironically, the same company seems to be responsible for the decimation of the honeybee population. The bee is the canary bird of our time.

If the bee dies off, we will soon follow. The spooky part of this story is that Monsanto just happens to be developing a genetically engineered bee strain to replace the bees destroyed by their chemicals.

Today the many fronts covered by the movement are legitimate targets and the movement should be thanked even though they don't have a centralized leadership, which many times looks like a detriment but seems to work for them quite well. They are however, easily infiltrated by Anarchists and thugs because of their loose structure.

Two and a half hours of talking or rather listening to my friend and I was dedicating myself to hours, no days of fact checking. He was completely right, as usual. Thornton promised to be back in a couple months. I said I would work on a new list of questions, maybe not so heavy next time.

For example, I have noticed that many girls and young women speak as though their statements are in the form of a question, you know like on Jeopardy. Watch the news sometime when they are interviewing some eyewitness sitting in her SUV.

"I saw the man hit the other man with a crow bar?" the inflection slides up at the end of each sentence.

This always perplexes me. They learned to speak in the same area I did?

We'll see how Thornton will tackle that one. Meanwhile I'll go back to my crossword.

"Hey, Honey, I'm almost done?"

Chapter Ten: MY FRIEND STAN

I hope that man's inhumanity to man does not start before birth because I can verify it continues throughout life and long after death. I usually write humorous pieces but I can truthfully say I can find no humor in this tale.

I have a friend. I must call my friend Stan for this piece. Stan was a likable person. Stan had many friends. Stan worked in an industry that helped many people and these people loved Stan for going above the norm for them.

Stan had many friends at the local bar where I hung out. Everyone has friends at a bar. A bar has a number of things built in that keep you coming back daily. Televisions, music, video games, KENO, great bargains on food and drink and the fellowship of other people are the threads that are woven together to make the spider web that is your bar. The bar owner or worker must carefully weave these fibers together to attract you and the others and yet follow the laws that the state puts in the way. If all these fibers are woven together in the right percentages, the whole web becomes invisible next to the big porch light in your neighborhood.

Bar patrons, like moths are not created equal. Some moths are more susceptible to the shinier things in a bar than other moths. A kind ear, cleaver conversation and the ubiquitous special drink concoction are the tools of the salivating bartender.

Unlike the real spider, the bartender's courtship does not end with a dance to the death. Remember, this has to happen again tomorrow. The bartender's work is to wrap the patron in a gossamer jacket of good feeling, and after the patron is completely relaxed and has fed the spider, the spider's children and debt holders, the moth is released back into the dark. Sometimes the patron has a safe way home, many times, no.

Stumbling out the door, the moth believes the spider is a moth's best friend and swears to return tomorrow. Check and mate!

This now gives the spider time to look for another corpulent moth.

Bills to pay!

Sometimes the spider and the moth are both convinced they love each other; maybe they can, in a lucid moment, actually see each other for what they really are and still somehow live with that. I don't know.

I know that when a susceptible moth is being played, the other moths can only watch the greedy dance in awe. No one will stop the torment, they can't. If they object to the treatment of other moths or suggest that they see the emperor's BVDs they can be sent out into the night based on the state laws the spider hides behind. The moth/spider dance has been stepped to by many since time began and since alcohol has been sold to moths everywhere.

My friend Stan was a moth, a very needy moth. Stan was also part firefly. Every spider in town could see Stan coming and knew the tastiness and how nutritious Stan's life fluids were. Every spider sated themselves on Stan's life fluids no matter how deflated Stan would be at the end of the feeding cycle. There came a point I could no longer watch, I sought another porch light. There was nothing I could do; moths can only do so much. The spiders seem to out-number us and there seems to be a secret pact among them to keep track of needy moths.

Last week Stan died. It was a terrible gruesome death. Fortunately, it had nothing to do with spiders or webs or work, it was an accident. Everyone was sad. Everyone forgot the abuse Stan took at the arms and fangs of the spiders.

Web lash marks and fang holes disappear when you die in many cases. Fortunately for Stan, this was the case. Why should everyone know of the moth in the closet when it is broad daylight and friends and family are in the room?

The room, this time, is in a funeral parlor. The room is packed to the point of needing additional chairs to be placed in the ante room. One hundred seventy five family members, friends and fellow moths gathered to see Stan off to a new dimension. I knew one moth that was secretly proud of Stan for surviving all the spider bites and glad Stan would no longer be part of the soup du jour at the Spiderville Bar and Grill. No longer could Stan be taken advantage of by the heartless. No longer could Stan be embarrassed in public by those who are only there to line their pockets with the money of the emotional and needy. I could never have been more wrong. Even after death, Stan is still being used. This time Stan was the shiny item that attracted one hundred seventy five red eyed, sense numbed true friends of Stan.

After all the friends and family had their turn tearfully telling their stories of youth and brotherhood, the good thoughts of the fallen are being used as a platform for the spider's spider. I used to have disdain for the spider. Now everyday spiders are being also rounded up and treated like moths. Who can trump the spider? Who can show no mercy to the one hundred seventy-five? Who can wring out the emotions of everyone to feed their agenda not only shamelessly but with a slurping noise that can be heard through the din of his own reedy voice?

For fifty minutes we cried and commiserated together for our loss. Now, for the next twenty, we have to pay for the ignorance of our grief. We came, thinking of Stan, from one hundred seventy-five different angles, one hundred seventy-five different points of view. We are now parts of a gigantic moth about to be sucked dry by the gigantic spider. This spider is now in control. This spider has laced up his web, gathered it together and holds all of us over his thirsty mouth. We will not be devoured yet. Nothing can stop what is happening in front of us and the spider knows it. We cannot escape. It would be a slur against our friend. The spider knows this and it only makes him hungrier.

"Jesus!"

I am not swearing. Jesus is the topic of this twenty minute infomercial. The spider of all spiders is a man of the cloth. This means no one has power over this spider. There are no brooms big enough. No boot heals hard enough to combat this spider in his own territory. He has the upper hand and he knows it. Beads of sweat are collecting on his brow. His fingers twitch in anticipation.

"Thank you, Lord, for providing such bounty I cannot wait to receive." I can hear him think. "One hundred seventy-five delicious butterflies are here to be fit with their terminal jackets and all for free! All for me! They paid me to be here. I am only a freelance parson, a rental; I have no church of my own."

So he has to work fast. He is testing himself.

"How many times can I say Jesus in twenty minutes? How many times can I talk Jesus up and down yet keep quoting the Old Testament? It doesn't matter. They can't argue with me, not in front of their dead friend. They can't point out that I'm talking out of my ass with real Jesus gibberish." He stops to wipe his brow. "Maybe I can say Jesus for every person here, ninety-eight, ninety-nine…"

For a person that didn't show a particular swing one way or another to Jesus, Stan was now being paired up with the Gentle Jew as though they were childhood chums.

It is now painfully clear to me. No matter how hard the bartender can suck money out of you and embarrass you in public by sending you out the door looking like a complete loser, the clergy can snap the wrinkles out of you and fluff you up to make you look like you couldn't wait to die to give him the chance to start talking about his favorite topic.

Even after death, you are fair game to the blood suckers, no matter how they disguise themselves.

About the Author

Jack lives in the Pacific Northwest with his wife Ruth. He is retired from the construction industry and likes to golf, bowl and write.